Take a Lesson in Drama

Take a Lesson in Drama

by Kate Smith

foulsham educational

LONDON • NEW YORK • TORONTO • SYDNEY

foulsham

The Publishing House, Bennetts Close,
Cippenham, Slough, Berks SL1 5AP England

ISBN 0-572-02275-1

Copyright © 1998 W. Foulsham & Co. Ltd.

Printed in Great Britain

English in the National Curriculum

The National Curriculum for English is concerned, above all, to develop in pupils the skills of effective communication – writing, speaking and listening – and to encourage them to be responsive in ways that are knowledgeable and enthusiastic.

Kate Smith has written *Take a Lesson in Drama* to reflect these requirements. As well as providing an accessible knowledge base suitable for introducing pupils to the world of theatre, she has also compiled a wealth of material to help pupils develop effective communication in speech and writing, and to challenge pupils to listen and respond to others with understanding. She introduces an element of fun into this process with the use of quizzes and imaginative activities, and encourages further research work to build on previous experience.

The great variety of units gives pupils the opportunity to focus on such key speaking and listening skills as:

- Telling stories – real or imaginary
- Using the imagination
- Exploring and developing ideas and themes
- Broadening vocabulary
- Presenting work to different audiences
- Listening with understanding
- Remembering specific points
- Improvising and performing
- Understanding appropriacy of language for a given situation
- Evaluating contributions
- Responding to a variety of stimuli

Take a Lesson in Drama involves pupils working with others and challenges them with a demanding range of activities that are exciting, interesting and related to their own experiences. The book reflects the requirements of the National Curriculum whilst providing a real source of imaginative material for use with all levels.

When and how to use this book

Designed to be used by literally *ANY* teacher, this book contains 73 carefully planned, practical, down-to-earth drama lessons for use with pupils from 9–16 years. All the lessons are easy to use and require no complicated resources or real expertise so even the most inexperienced teacher can use them with confidence. All in all, this book will prove an invaluable aid to the non-specialist who suddenly finds drama somehow included on his timetable; the less experienced drama teacher who needs help for those first few weeks and the teacher who suddenly needs to cover a drama lesson for a sick colleague; it may possibly provide even specialists with some new ideas.

In practical terms, that means this book can be used to relieve all the headaches of preparing drama work when

a. The normal teacher is absent and a colleague has to cover the lesson.

b. The non-specialist or new teacher needs help to cope with the first few lessons.

c. The teacher has to leave the class for some reason.

d. Maternity leave, for example, means setting work for classes over a long period of time.

e. Exams and other school activities mean sudden classroom sessions in 'quiet' areas.

f. Even the specialist drama teacher's mind goes blank!

Contents

Age Chart

Activity	Age range
Ideas from Props	10–16
Mixed Worksheet	13–16
In a Different Time	11–16
Faces	9–16
Greek Theatre	11–16
Quick Crossword	11–14
Brief Encounters	9–12
Assess Your Performance	11–16
Practical Skills	9–16
Rearrange the Jobs	9–12
Diagram of the Stage	11–16
Lost!	10–13
What Production?	9–16
Build a Character	11–16
Design a Poster	10–13
The Party	13–16
Write a Play	9–16
Ideas Contest	9–16
Medieval Drama	11–14
Your Views	14–16
Colours	9–16
Shakespearean Theatre	12–16
The Designer	12–16
Using the Phone	11–13
General Theatre Quiz	10–16
Somewhere Different	9–16
Stage and Screen Review	11–14
Lighting	14–16
Take a Proverb	9–16
Victorian Theatre	13–16
Making Sounds	9–13
Choose a Title	9–16
Foreign Parts	11–14
Mime	9–12
Stage Set	9–16

Activity	Age range
	9 · 10 · 11 · 12 · 13 · 14 · 15 · 16
Odd Words	9 — 16
Statues	9 — 13
The Problem	12 — 16
Imagination Stretchers	9 — 16
One Word Story Plays	14 — 16
Persuasion	9 — 16
Strange Phrases	12 — 15
Thief, Drunkard, Liar!	14 — 16
Puppets	9 — 13
Myths and Legends	10 — 14
Improvisation from Titles	9 — 16
Odd Shoes	9 — 16
Freeze!	9 — 16
Over the Wall	9 — 16
Play for Today	14 — 16
Looking Down	11 — 16
Trapped	11 — 16
Cheese Fugue	10 — 13
Set a Scene	11 — 16
Headlines	12 — 16
The Interview	12 — 16
Don't Just Sit There	13 — 16
Survivor	15 — 16
Round the Circle	9 — 16
Five Stages of a Life	12 — 16
It All Goes Wrong	11 — 16
Never Say Die	9 — 16
Take Your Pick	9 — 16
Sculptures	10 — 13
Effects of Mood	11 — 16
Who Dunnit?	11 — 16
John Court Case	14 — 16 / 13 — 16
Expression	14 — 16

Ideas from Props

Pupils should be able to work quietly on their own with little or no assistance. This exercise helps them to be more imaginative and original in their drama work and is suitable for any age group between 10–16 years.

Suggest five ways in which each of the following props could be used as the basis for a short play or improvisation.

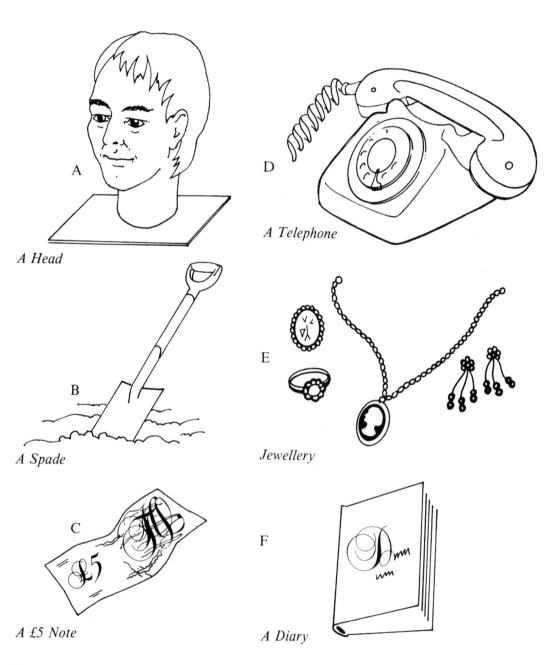

A

A Head

B

A Spade

C

A £5 Note

D

A Telephone

E

Jewellery

F

A Diary

Mixed Worksheet

Pupils will need plain and lined paper, pens and pencils for this lesson, which is most suitable for pupils aged between 13–16 years who have had SOME instruction (and possible experience) in production.

A.   Describe a scene which would go with each of these 'sets'.

a.

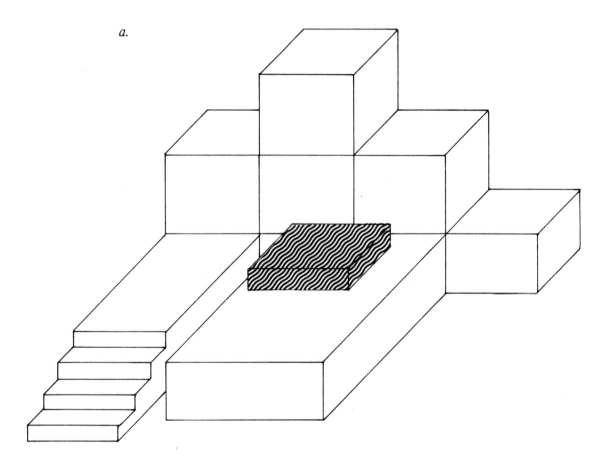

b.

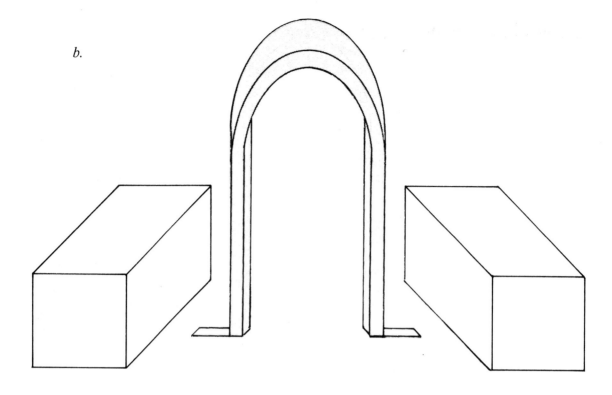

B. Describe a scene to go with each of these different lightings.

    a. One red spotlight in middle of empty stage.

    b. Two white spotlights anywhere on stage.

    c. Mixture of green and red general lighting.

    d. General bright lighting.

    e. Blue lighting generally.

C. Draw just the face or even the whole body to show each of these characters.

    a. Witch or devil.

    b. A fat landlady.

    c. Someone from outer space.

    d. Any character from the past.

    e. Drunken man or tramp.

In a Different Time

Designed to make pupils use their imagination, this lesson requires little or no help from the teacher after the introduction, and is generally suitable for all ages between 11–16 although some less able groups may need extra guidance.

INTRODUCTION (to be read to the class)
An interesting idea can sometimes be made even more interesting if set in a different place or time than usual.

For instance, the idea of someone receiving bad news might be made more effective if it is set in a war time sketch. Similarly, 'the problem' could probably be worked into a more original improvisation if set in the past or even the future instead of the present.

Think carefully about different periods of history, about the future, about different times of the day or in people's lives. Now think carefully about your own drama work over the past year.

Look at the different 'times' given below. Write out two really good ideas for an improvisation for each of them.

a. *World War I or II*

b. *The 1920s*

c. *The future*

d. *Midnight*

e. *Old age*

f. *The Victorian times*

g. *The Stone Age*

h. *Dawn*

Faces

This face has been carefully drawn so that it can be used in a variety of ways by both girls and boys aged 9–16 years. Tracing paper, plain paper, pencils and coloured pens are of course a 'must' for this lesson.

1. Use tracing paper to copy this face onto paper. The face has been left as plain as possible to allow you greater freedom of interpretation and design.

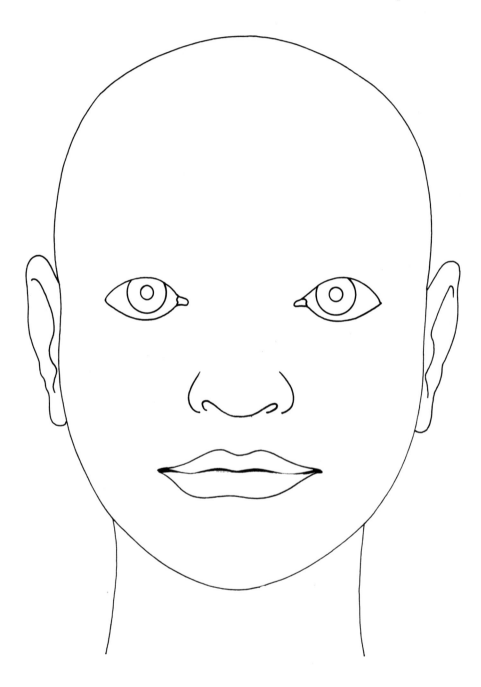

2. Now, using as much imagination as possible, make up this face to look like a witch or spy or an alien or an old man or an Arabian princess or . . . any idea that you may have. Coloured pencils or felt tips are ideal.

Greek Theatre

It makes sense that all drama pupils should, at some point, learn about how all drama began. At what particular age depends upon the individual class and teacher. This lesson has, therefore, been written very simply and clearly so that it can be easily understood and used, in some way, with all pupils aged 11 – 16 years.

Younger pupils will probably be more interested if the passage is read to them by the teacher, allowing for interspersed comments and questions. They will enjoy doing the questions and drawings afterwards.

Older pupils may well find the questions rather too easy but can nevertheless benefit from reading the information, especially if they need to know something of Greek drama as part of an examination course. Pupils will of course need paper and pens for this quiet work.

GREEK THEATRE – THE PLAYS

All drama began in Greece thousands of years ago. The Greeks were performing plays about 500 years before Christ was born and before Julius Caesar even thought about coming to Britain.

The ancient Greeks believed in many different Gods and one of these was the God of wine and fertility called Dionysus. Each year, in the Spring, a great festival was held in honour of Dionysus and everyone would stop work and travel to Athens for the celebrations and religious ceremonies.

The festival lasted several days and, as well as singing, dancing, poetry and rituals, there was a great play competition. Every year three well-known Greek dramatists would compete to see who could produce the best play. The plays were usually about the Gods or Greek heroes and told the stories of great Greek myths or legends. There would be very few actors but the plays always included a 'chorus' of about fifteen identically dressed people. Their job was to provide crowd scenes where necessary, sing and dance, comment upon the play and generally help tell the story. The plays were often very long and did not include much action at first. Violence and deaths were never acted out in front of the audience so either the chorus or a messenger had to report these events.

At first, all Greek plays were tragedies or serious plays but eventually comedies were introduced at these festivals too. Many of the ancient Greek plays have survived through the centuries and are still being performed today. One Greek dramatist called Sophocles wrote many tragedies and about seven of these are still known. His play 'Oedipus' is perhaps the most famous. This tells the story of how, when the King and Queen of Thebes have a son, a strange prediction is made that the boy will grow up to kill his father and marry his mother. On hearing this, the King decides to get rid of his son, Oedipus, by leaving him on a mountain side to die. Oedipus is discovered by a shepherd, however, who brings him up as his own son. Many years later, Oedipus does unknowingly kill his true father, the King, and then goes to the city, now ruled by his uncle. The city is threatened by a sinister monster that no one seems able to destroy. In desperation, an announcement is made that whoever manages to rid the city of this terrible monster will be rewarded by marrying the beautiful widow of the old King and so becoming the new King and ruler. Oedipus succeeds in killing the monster and so, without knowing it, ends up marrying his own mother. Later, when he finds out his true identity and realises what he has done, Oedipus unhappily tears out his eyes and the Queen hangs herself.

Another of Sophocles' sad plays is called 'Antigone'. Antigone's father, the King, dies and one of her two brothers becomes the new King. However, when the second brother hears this, he returns to attack the city and overthrows the first. Sadly, both brothers are killed in this battle and so Antigone's uncle, Creon, a just and kind man, has to become the ruler.

To prevent further attacks on the country he rules that one of the brothers shall receive an honourable funeral while the other will be left to rot on the street as an enemy of the State deserves. Anyone attempting to move or bury this body would be sentenced to death.

His own niece, Antigone, is so determined that both her brothers should get a proper burial, she deliberately tries to disobey this order and gets arrested. Creon tries to reason with her but Antigone remains stubbornly determined to succeed in giving her brother a proper funeral service even though her own life is at risk. Creon sadly decides he must keep to his ruling and Antigone is put to death.

The Theatres

The early Greek theatres were not at all like our theatres today. Greece is a warm country so the plays were performed out in the open countryside. The audience would sit on rows of seats carved into the hillsides in a huge semi-circle and down below, at the bottom of the slopes, a flat piece of land provided an area for singing and dancing, and for the chorus, called the 'orkestra' (orchestra). Just behind this, there was a raised platform or stage where the actors performed the main play. This was known as the 'proskenion', a word which still describes some modern stages.

About 20,000 people could be seated in the audience of these huge open air theatres and yet even those seated at the back, far up above the actors, could hear every word of the play quite clearly because the sides of the hills naturally echoed and amplified the sound of the actors' voices.

To make it easier for the audience far above to see the actors clearly, padding was sometimes added to the costumes to make the actors look bigger, and platform shoes were worn to make them appear taller. Facial expressions like crying or smiling cannot easily be seen from a distance, so all the actors, including the chorus, wore masks and wigs to help show their characters and feelings. Their masks also had specially shaped mouthpieces which amplified the sound of their voices. Wearing masks also meant that each actor could play more than one part in the play. A place was needed to store these masks and other props and where the actors could change masks quickly. A small building called the skene was therefore built at the edge of the proskenion (stage). At first this was a wooden type of shed but later it was built of stone and beautifully decorated. It was then used as part of the play just as scenery is used today. Actors pretending to be Gods could be lowered from the top of the skene and others could enter or exit using this building.

Many words we use in drama today came from the early Greek Dramas. 'Dialogue' was a Greek word meaning 'talk' or 'backchat' –'Drama' meant 'thing done' – 'Mime' meant 'imitate' – a 'theatre' was a 'seeing place' and 'Audience' meant 'people hearing'.

GREEK THEATRE – QUESTIONS AND WORK

1. Copy out this diagram of a Greek theatre.

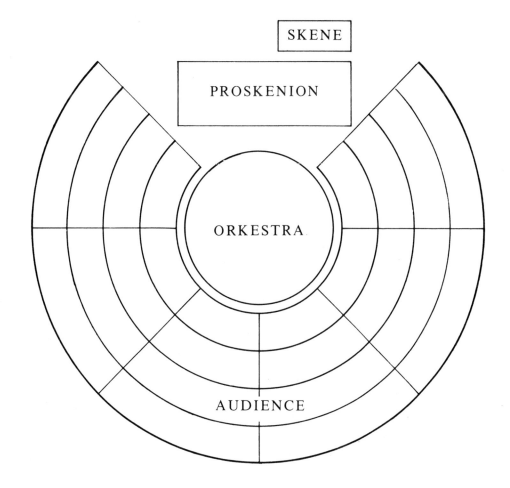

2. Draw a Greek mask showing sadness, horror, evil or happiness.

3. Answer the following questions:–

A. Who wrote the play 'Oedipus'?

   a. Sophocles
   b. Antigone
   c. Dionysus

B. Why was it easy to hear the actors from so far above?

   a. They used microphones.

   b. The hillsides naturally amplified the sounds.

   c. Loudspeakers were placed among the audience.

C. How many dramatists competed in the festival's Drama competition?

   a. 2

   b. 5

   c. 3

D. The skene was a building to provide:

   a. Refreshments in the interval?

   b. An actors' changing room?

   c. A public entrance to the theatre?

E. The actors acted the play on:

   a. The hillsides?

   b. The orkestra?

   c. The proskenion?

F. The audience sat:

   a. On the hilltops?

   b. In the skene?

   c. On seats carved into the hillside?

   d. On benches indoors?

G. Which of the following are true?

   a. Actors wore platform shoes.

   b. Actors wore masks.

c. Most early plays were comedies.

d. Early plays told stories of Gods and heroes.

e. The chorus helped tell the story.

f. It was possible for each actor to play more than one part.

Quick Crossword

A fairly easy theatre crossword, perhaps reproduced on the board, most suitable for pupils aged 11 – 14 years.

Across

2. Place where plays are acted. (Theatre)
5. Object used in a play. (Prop)
6. Raised floor which actors perform on. (Stage)
10. Practices for a performance. (Rehearsals)
11. People found in a play. (Characters)

Down

1. Play with a sad ending. (Tragedy)
3. Female who takes part in a play. (Actress)
4. What actors wear. (Costume)
5. Remind actors of forgotten lines. (Prompt)
7. Structure(s) built on stage to show setting. (Scenery)
8. The words of the play used by the actors in rehearsal. (Script)
9. The things performed. (Plays).

Brief Encounters

This lesson aims to help younger pupils develop their imagination and is therefore most suitable for those aged 9–12 years, although it could easily be adapted for use with slightly older classes. Pupils will need paper and pens and should work quietly on their own or in pairs.

1. Give six examples of different types of meeting as shown below. Try to include interesting characters and places.

    eg; Mrs Brown met a ghost in her bedroom.

    ....met/meets....................in/at ....

2. Now choose two of these examples or perhaps think of a new idea and complete the following simple story outlines.

    a. .... meets .... at ....and they...............
        ....then goes to.....................where he or she sees
        .... However,..................... turns up and so ....

    b. ....goes ....where he/she ....He/she then
        meets.....................and .... They ....Eventu-
        ally,.....................tells .... about.......................and in the
        end...............

3. If there is still time, quickly write your own outline for a play which centres around a brief encounter/meeting.

Assess Your Performance

This lesson should help develop a sense of self-criticism in drama work. Suitable for all pupils aged 11–16 years, although it may be of particular value to those pupils taking examination drama courses. The personal lists will be written on paper or in their own notebooks.

1. Think about any recent improvisation/acting work you have done in drama lessons. Give an account of what you did – on your own, in pairs or as a group.

2. Look at the chart below. This shows some of the things that can go wrong with group sketches or improvisations in class. Select any of the points which applied to your drama work during the lesson you have described in (1). Write down your own list.

Everyone speaking at same time.

Speaking too quietly or mumbling words.

Showed lack of concentration by giggling.

Too much moving around.

Not enough variation of movements, therefore boring.

Had good idea but too difficult for group.

One person in group took over all the important acting bits.

You didn't manage to complete your work.

You ran out of ideas.

No real atmosphere or mood was created.

Couldn't keep in character throughout.

Plot (storyline) was a bit boring.

Plot was a bit childish or silly.

Acting was hesitant and awkward.

Plot was not very easy to follow.

Someone/something put you off.

Group arguments over what to do.

Play was too short or too long.

3. Now, using your own list as a guideline, write a couple of paragraphs assessing what went wrong with the group's, and your own, acting during the lesson. Say also how you could have improved your drama work in some way. Mention, too, anything that you felt was good about it. You may, after all, have produced some excellent improvisation work and if this is the case you will enjoy writing about what made it so successful.

Practical Skills and Talents Questionnaire

The information this questionnaire gives about individual pupils' hopes, skills and talents is immensely useful when planning any type of school production. It helps prevent the same pupils being used all the time while others feel missed out; it immediately shows which pupils have had some previous stage experience as well as those who are dying to have a go, and it provides hard-pressed production staff with a ready list of pupils willing to lend a hand with all manner of production chores, be it designing posters or showing parents to their seats.

Permission is granted by the Publisher to the teacher to photostat the questionnaire for classroom use.

QUESTIONNAIRE

1. Do you enjoy acting?   YES   NO

2. Do you belong to a Drama club?   YES   NO
                                                                                        USED TO
   Which club? ....

3. How often do you attend?   REGULARLY/SOMETIMES/SELDOM

4. Have you ever acted at a public performance?   YES   NO
   If *yes*   when..
               where...
               character(s)..
               play ....
   If *no* would you like to take part in a public performance? YES   NO

5. Which type of acting suits you best?   SERIOUS/COMEDY/ANY

6. Which would you prefer, given the chance?   LEAD PART/SMALL
                                                                              PART/CHORUS

7. Would you feel confident enough to audition in front of
   others?   YES   NO

8. How would you find rehearsing at lunchtimes or after
   school?   EASY   DIFFICULT

9. Name any time you would *never* be able to attend rehearsals.
   ....

10. Do you enjoy dancing?   YES   NO

11. Do you attend a) Dance club?   YES   NO
                                                                                    USED TO
                          b) Dance lessons?   YES   NO
                                                                                    USED TO

12. What type(s) of dancing do you enjoy/perform well? Please tick.

    a. Tap

    b. Ballet

    c. Robotics

    d. Modern

22

    e. Disco

    f. Latin American

    g. Ballroom

    h. Majorettes

    i. Anything energetic – musical
        type.

13. Have you ever danced on stage in a public performance?   IN A GROUP
                                                                 SOLO
                                                                 NEVER
    Would you like to?   YES NO

14. Do you enjoy singing?   YES NO

15. If *yes* would you enjoy singing   IN A LARGE GROUP/SOLO/
                                                   SMALL GROUP

16. Do you play any musical instrument(s)?
    Name it or them...
    How well do you play?   VERY WELL/QUITE GOOD/O.K./POOR

17. Please tick any of the following skills that you particularly enjoy.

    a. Photography

    b. Hairdressing/design

    c. Decorative forms of writing

    d. Painting

    e. Drawing

    f. Woodwork

    g. Sewing

    h. Costume making/designing

    i. Typing

    j. Designing posters

    k. Making objects out of card or
        scraps

    l. Lighting

18. Are you able to complete design/art/practical work quickly?   YES   NO

19. Are you able and prepared to take on practical work:

    a. At home?   YES   NO   LACK MATERIALS

    b. At lunchtimes?   YES NO

20. Would you like to work 'Backstage' for a school
    production if asked?   YES NO
    If *yes* what sort of backstage work would you enjoy?

    ....

21. Do you feel you are able to perform any of the following quite well?
    Please tick.

    a. Acrobatics

    b. Juggling

    c. Magic tricks

    d. Telling jokes really well

    e. Impressions

    f. Read a passage loudly, clearly
        and with expression

    g. Mime

    h. Others

22. Give details of any specific talents or skills you have which you may feel
    have not already been included in this questionnaire.

    ....

    ....

Rearrange the Jobs

*Suitable for pupils aged 9–12 years, this very simple theatre puzzle should prove
informative as well as amusing. As the exercise is very short it is ideal for those
times when the lesson has been somehow drastically shortened or when you need to
leave the class for a few minutes. Pupils will need paper to write on.*

Rearrange and write out the following so that each job in the theatre is placed
opposite its correct description.

Stage Manager	arranges dances.
Prompt	sells tickets.
Choreographer	calls the actors.
Director	in charge of lighting.
Call girl/boy	in charge of making sure
everything that happens on

	stage goes smoothly during performance.
Lighting Manager	helps with forgotten lines during performance.
Box Office	rehearses actors and is generally in charge of production.

Diagram of the Stage

This simple, quick and instructive exercise for pupils aged 11 – 16 years is ideal for those times when the lesson has been somehow shortened or you need to leave the class for a few minutes knowing they have something sensible to do. Plain paper and pencils are needed.

Copy out this diagram and try to remember what the different parts of the stage are called. Rehearsals for a school or club play are a lot easier if you know what the director means when he asks you to come 'downstage'.

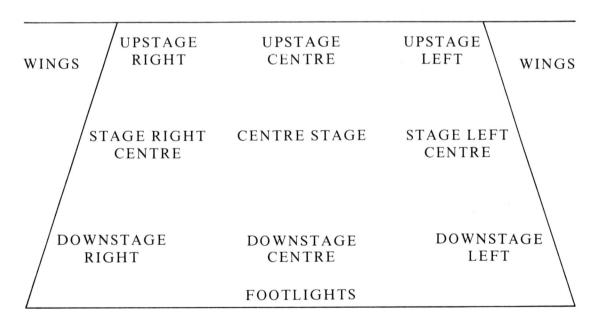

Lost!

This short lesson or part of a lesson (10–15 mins) is most suitable for pupils aged 10–13 years. They will need writing materials.

1. Make a quick list of 12 items or 'things' you might lose either at home or outside.

2. Now think of what else you might lose or be lost in any way, other than objects or things. List 6 ideas.

3. Have you gained any interesting ideas for a play from either of your two lists? If so – perhaps you can work on these in one of your other drama lessons.

What Production?

This easy written work enables pupils to write about the plays that they, personally, enjoy and is suitable for all pupils aged 9–16 years. Paper and pens are obviously needed.

1. Write a short list of any plays, large or small, that you have seen or been involved in since you began school.

2. Write a couple of paragraphs (about 100 words) describing any one of these productions.

3. What play or musical would you like to see performed at your school? Write two paragraphs explaining what the play is about and why you think it would be a good production.

Build a Character

This lesson aims to help pupils aged 11–16 years overcome the easy temptation to use stereotypes rather than rounded or convincing characters in their plays. Pupils will need paper and pens to create as many interesting characters as they can in the time allowed. These could be used, perhaps, in future drama work.

1. Take one 'character' from List A. Now choose one item from List B and then as many items as you wish from the boxes below to build up a full description or story for that 'character'. E.g: – Father of two children – works in a large office – always working and very ambitious, normally quiet but sometimes bad tempered, has one particular problem and needs to make a decision. He meets an interesting person and has a piece of good luck.

Remember – there is no right or wrong way of doing this – just use your imagination to build up an interesting character.

List A

1. Mother/father of two children.

2. Elderly person.

3. Young person

4. Teenager living at home.

5. Middle aged man or woman.

6. Young mum/dad with small baby.

List B

1. Hospital worker.

2. On the dole.

3. Works in a large office.

4. At school/college.

5. Just started new job some-where.

6. Has very hard and tiring job.

7. Works in a busy shop.

8. Stays at home through choice.

9. Self employed.

10. Has well-paid, fairly glamorous job.

11. About to be made redundant.

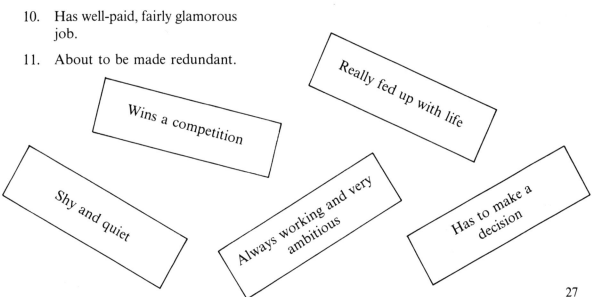

Really fed up with life

Wins a competition

Shy and quiet

Always working and very ambitious

Has to make a decision

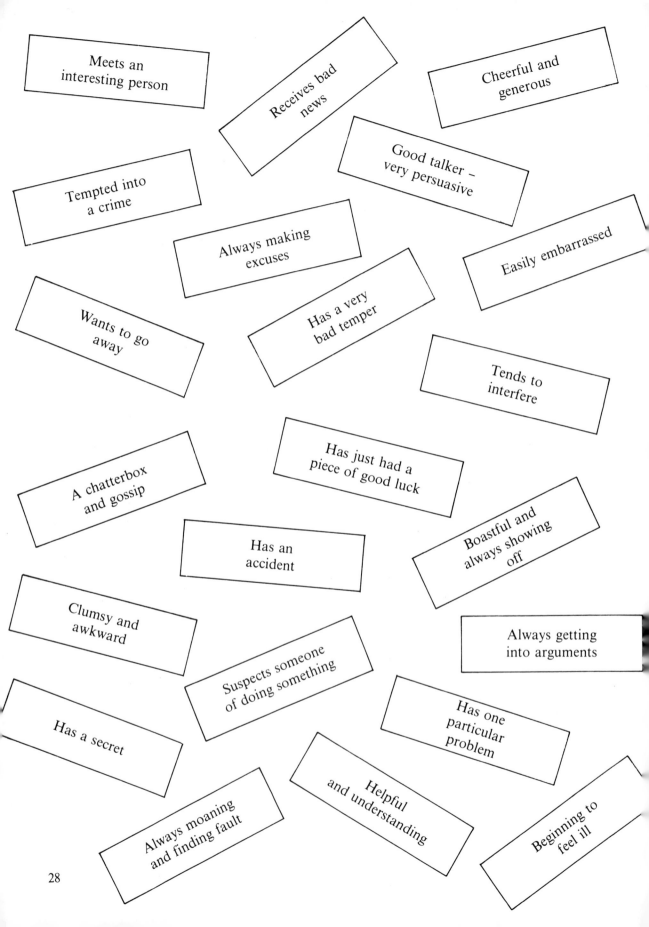

Meets an interesting person

Receives bad news

Cheerful and generous

Tempted into a crime

Good talker – very persuasive

Always making excuses

Easily embarrassed

Wants to go away

Has a very bad temper

Tends to interfere

A chatterbox and gossip

Has just had a piece of good luck

Boastful and always showing off

Has an accident

Clumsy and awkward

Always getting into arguments

Suspects someone of doing something

Has one particular problem

Has a secret

Always moaning and finding fault

Helpful and understanding

Beginning to feel ill

Design a Poster

Most suitable for pupils aged 10–13 years. This lesson involves design work for a given play and therefore plain paper, pencils and coloured pens will be needed.

1.   Think about any play you have read, watched or heard of. It may be a play you have read as a class in drama or English lessons, for example, or a well known musical.

2.   Now do the following:-

     a.   List the main characters.

     b.   Describe or draw the opening scene.

     c.   Design a poster advertising this play.

The Party

This exercise helps pupils appreciate different points of view about a modern social problem and could be used as part of their work on characterisation or as an introduction to 'social drama'. The lesson is most suitable for pupils aged 13–16 years who will, of course, need paper and pens.

1.   Think about the following situation:-
     'Mum and dad go out one evening leaving their teenage son or daughter to watch TV, do some homework and go to bed as normal. While they are gone, a few friends of the son/daughter phone up and arrange to come round for an hour or so. Unfortunately, one or two of them bring round yet more friends and a small party takes place which goes on until quite late. Everyone seems to be enjoying themselves and someone, unknown to the son or daughter, has brought drinks and cigarettes. The parents arrive back earlier than expected and are horrified by what they see. They order everyone to leave immediately and severely punish their son/daughter who is equally upset by their reaction.'

2.   Now write out the following, clearly showing each person's different view of what has happened.

     a.   Conversation between mother and father either the same evening or the next morning. (Which may be quite different).

     b.   Mum or dad telling one of the neighbours or a workmate about their shock and horror at discovering the party.

     c.   Conversation between the son or daughter and one of their friends the next day.

d. Possible argument that follows immediately between the parents and their son or daughter.

Write a Play

Classes will need lined paper and pens for this very simple lesson which can be used with all pupils aged 9–16 years. If possible – follow up this work by getting the class to elect two trustworthy pupils to be judges.

1. Choose one of the titles given below and write a short play based on that title. It doesn't really matter if you do not finish it by the end of the lesson provided you have established the main characters and plot of your play.

   Make sure it is set out properly:–

   e.g: *Scene 2*

   John and Mark are just leaving school . . .

   John: Are you coming to the football match tomorrow?

   Mark: Yeah, I think so. Oh hang on a minute, mum said something about everyone staying in tomorrow. (*He pulls a face.*) My grandparents are coming to stay, worse luck!

   John: (*Laughing.*) That'll be fun for you! Still, your mum will probably let you come anyway. (*They arrive near John's road.*) Look – I've got to go – see you tomorrow if you can make it. Bye!

Titles:

1. Danger

2. The wrong place

3. Too late

4. The journey

5. The secret

6. The restaurant

Ideas Contest

Suitable for all classes aged 9–16 years, this simple lesson encourages pupils to be quick thinking and imaginative in a way that is fun. You will need to give out paper, be prepared for some talking (they work in threes) and be ready to time each section of the contest before finally having to decide upon a class winner. If there is time, ask all the 'winners' to read out their work and then choose one 'class winner' from them; either the one with the most words used from the list OR perhaps the best sketch outline.

1. Study the words below.

VAN	CHOCOLATE
HELP	BEARD
DOG	KITCHEN
MAP	FRIDAY
BOTTLE	SHY
BOOK	DESK
LOVE	VIOLENT
TOMORROW	NEVER

TROUBLE	SCHOOL
ROPE	WINDOW
BLIND	NEW CARPET
HOLIDAY	RING
DINNER	THEFT
FIRE	SECRET
ANGEL	BUILDING SITE
PICTURE	HAIRCUT

2. Pick out any three words from the list and put them together in any way you wish, to form an idea for a drama sketch. Write out a brief summary of your ideas. *You are allowed no more than 10 minutes for this.*

3. When you have finished get together with two other people and swap papers or books twice so that you each read each others' summaries. Decide who had the best idea for a sketch from the words they chose.

4. Now look at the long list of 32 words. Using only three words should have proved fairly easy, but now try and build up another outline of a drama

sketch or 'improvisation' *using as many words as possible* from the above list. Once again, write out your ideas showing how they build up to an interesting sketch and note the number of words you have been able to use, at the bottom. You are allowed 20 minutes for this.

5. Work in competition with the other two pupils whose ideas you read before and see who can use the most words sensibly and effectively.

6. At the end of twenty minutes – read each others' work as before and elect a 'winner' from your trio: i.e. the one with the most words used.

Medieval Drama

The information given below is easy to read and understand so that pupils aged between 11–14 years should have little difficulty in quietly completing the written work that follows. You may feel that older pupils too, possibly those taking a drama examination course, would benefit from this lesson but do warn them – they might find the language and questions rather simple! Classes will, of course, need paper, pens and perhaps coloured pencils for this work.

A. Read the following information about Drama in Medieval times.

How it all began:
Drama in Britain began in the middle ages or medieval period. The first 'plays' were performed in the churches and were really just a few lines from the bible acted out by priests to make the services more interesting and help the congregation to understand the bible stories better. In those days, church services were spoken in Latin and very few ordinary people would be able to understand this, so acting out small scenes really helped.

These church 'plays' became very popular and soon ordinary people started acting out scenes from the bible, at other times, in the courtyards and in the streets. Of course, not all the bible stories were very interesting so people began to alter them slightly, put in humorous bits and include more dramatic scenes with the devil and so on. Acting and plays became more and more a popular part of everyday life in many towns; as did acrobatics, singing and music which were also performed in the streets at this time.

Eventually, the powerful 'guilds' (the word 'guildhall' is still used today) in each town decided to set up and finance proper acting groups and organise much larger and more efficiently produced plays. The most famous of these were the 'Mystery Cycle plays' described below. Of course, as time passed, so each guild wanted to have better productions than others and so more time and money were spent on more elaborate costume and scenery. Plays too, were changed and included mime, comedy and acrobatics or dancing, to make them more entertaining.

Later still, acting groups, such as the one Shakespeare was involved in, either toured the country performing their own plays or set up the first real theatres in Britain . . . but that is explained more fully in the section 'Shakespearean Theatre'.

The different types of Medieval Drama:

1. *Church Plays* — Earliest plays in Britain. Short and simple. Monks, priests and choirboys acted out pieces from the bible.

2. *Street Plays* — Ordinary people acted out bible stories in the streets. Acrobats, musicians and clowns also performed in the streets.

3. *Mystery Cycle Plays* — The trade guilds took over. Many of the scenes and stories of the bible were put together to form one long play. The play was performed on carts which passed through the narrow streets of the town in order. Each cart showed a different scene and the people watched from their windows as each cart passed – eventually making up the whole story or play. Different trades or guilds were responsible for each scene. For example, the fishermen would do 'Noah's Ark' and the shepherds would organise the 'shepherds' scene' from the Nativity story and so on. The most famous Mystery Cycle plays were produced in York, Coventry and Chester and these are still being performed today.

4. *Miracle Plays* — These were short plays which told of miraculous events in the lives of their favourite saints: e.g: 'Play of St Catherine'.

5. *Morality Plays* — These were plays to show how man is weak and easily tempted by evil and the devil but he is always saved by 'Good' in the end. In other words, these plays had a 'moral' in them. 'Everyman' is one example of a medieval morality play that has been passed down through the centuries and is still being performed occasionally today.

B. *Questions*:

1. In what type of building were the first plays acted?

2. When these plays and acting became quite popular, who took over organising, training and paying for actors and plays?

3. What sort of things were these plays about?

4. How were the religious plays made more interesting?

5. When the Mystery Cycle plays were performed in the narrow street;
    a. What were used as stages?

    b. How was each scene shown separately?

    c. Where would the people watch from?

6. Name one city still famous for its Mystery Cycle Play.

7. What was the difference between Morality plays and Miracle plays?

8. Name any character which might be included in a Medieval play.

C. Make notes for a short morality play suitable for today's audiences. Remember it is basically good triumphing over evil or a story with a little moral in it. Try to complete the writing at home.

D. Trace the picture overleaf onto your paper and then draw in a medieval scene from a Mystery Cycle play where there is presently an empty 'stage'. Stories from the bible or a scene with the devil may be suitable.

Your Views

Pupils will need lined paper and pens for this quite advanced written work which is most suitable for pupils aged 14–16 years.

Choose one of the following 2 titles and write a sensible, clear essay expressing your own views on the topic chosen. Be absolutely honest and write forcefully. Your ideas may be very useful to the reader(s).

1. "Young people watch television, hire videos and go to the cinema but they *don't* go to the theatre". Do you feel this is a true statement? If so, why do you think theatre has little appeal to teenagers and what can theatres do to improve this situation?

2. Briefly describe drama lessons at your school and explain fully why you either enjoy or dislike them. If you do enjoy drama – give further details of your interests and experiences in this subject – both within school and outside.

Colours

Provided with paper and pens, pupils aged 9–16 years should have no difficulty using these colours as a stimulus for interesting ideas and written work.

Possible follow up: group improvisation work using the ideas given for the various colours, or give each group a different colour and ask them to create a short play.

1. Often we associate colours with certain moods, feelings, settings, ideas or things. Think of the following colours . . . what do they make you think of? RED . . . YELLOW . . . GREEN . . . WHITE . . . GREY . . . BLACK.

2. Copy out these circles being careful to copy the right number of spokes for each one. Now write a different idea against each of the spokes. The first one is partly done for you.

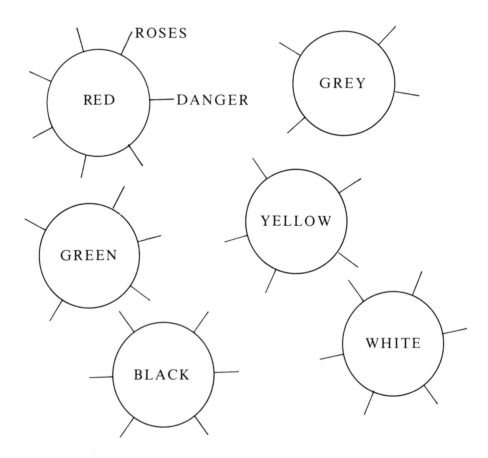

3. Choose any two ideas that you associate with different colours and write a couple of paragraphs on each explaining how they might be used to produce some interesting drama work. Don't just tell a story, use your imagination to decide upon appropriate characters, setting, time, lighting and so on.

Shakespearean Theatre

You may wish to read the passage through with the class before allowing them to complete the written work on their own. This lesson is generally suitable for all pupils aged 12–16 years, although you may wish to omit some exercises for use with younger pupils. Obviously paper is required for this work.

Shakespeare

William Shakespeare was born in Stratford upon Avon, Warwickshire in 1564 and was probably educated at Stratford Grammar School. He married Anne Hathaway in 1582. He has no direct descendants today because although he had two daughters and a son, the boy died quite young and the daughters had no children themselves.

Shakespeare soon began working with actors in London and then earned a reputation as a good playwright. Due to the Plague striking, acting stopped in London for a while and Shakespeare left. However, he later returned and joined with a leading company of actors called the 'Chamberlain's Men'. This name was then changed to the 'King's Men' and the group was known to be the best in London. They became quite prosperous and had the Globe Theatre built. This was later destroyed by fire but then rebuilt.

By 1597 Shakespeare was famous and very rich. He bought a huge house in Stratford and continued to write his plays. He stayed with the same acting company all his working life, eventually retired and died in Stratford in 1623.

Shakespeare is still known today as one of the greatest playwrights who ever lived and his many plays are still being acted all over the world.

These are just some of the famous plays he wrote:–

COMEDIES
The Merchant of Venice.
As You Like It.
Twelfth Night.
The Taming of the Shrew.
Much Ado About Nothing.
A Midsummer Night's Dream.
All's Well That Ends Well.

TRAGEDIES
Macbeth.
Hamlet.
Romeo and Juliet.
King Lear.
Antony and Cleopatra.
Othello.

HISTORICAL PLAYS:– King John, Richard III, Henry VI (parts 1, 2, 3.)

ACTING AND THEATRES OF THE TIME

After a while the guilds that had controlled and organised actors during the Medieval times began to lose their power. Private touring groups of actors began to travel in companies from town to town performing their own plays. Several important changes took place. These actors needed more space and freedom to act their plays and so, instead of using a series of small carts to act on, they began to build big stages in the yards of local inns and invited the audience to come to them to watch. They would play trumpets and have drummers to announce that they were about to start and the audience would come to watch them. Ordinary people would pay one penny and just stand in the yard. Richer people could pay to watch from the windows and galleries of the inns.

These courtyards were good places to act from because the actors could sometimes make use of existing windows and doors. Many rich people travelled very slowly from one town to another using carriages and horses and often stopped there for refreshment, so there was usually quite a large audience. There was no shelter for most of the audience though, so if it rained or was very cold both they and the actors suffered. The crowds were noisy and rough, so plays had to be good enough to make them want to listen and watch quietly.

Most actors were treated as rogues and tramps because they travelled and because acting was not a steady, respectable job. There were no women on the stage; boys played all the female parts. However, plays were quite a popular entertainment at that time and, as in earlier times, the people believed in the supernatural. Therefore they enjoyed plays that involved witches and ghosts and devils, and scenes that showed man's weaknesses, with murders and revenge.

Shakespeare is, of course, the most famous playwright of this time and his plays often had elements of the supernatural in them or were about man's wickedness. In MACBETH there is murder, three witches and Banquo's ghost; in HAMLET the main character sees the ghost of his murdered father and decides to seek revenge. Another famous playwright, Christopher Marlowe, wrote the very successful legend of a man who sells his soul to the devil for power and an easy life. Again the devil and evil spirits are used. Plays were therefore often quite violent and many people used to get hurt when large fights were performed. The audience was so close, they almost took part. At the end of many plays several characters would all die at once, which even today can be very funny if not done well. Naturally people enjoyed having a laugh too and so comedies were also performed.

Eventually, some actors became employed by the rich to entertain them and their guests and so acted constantly in one place. Other touring groups made enough money to set up permanent theatres where large audiences paid well. The first theatre was built in London by James Burbage and later the famous Globe Theatre of Shakespeare's company was built. The early theatres were styled like the inn courtyards with a large thrust stage, a spacious area for the audience to stand in and galleries overlooking the stage. They still had no roof and were not comfortable like modern theatres. Spectators would pay a penny to stand on the ground and two or three pence to go in the gallery. Sometimes rich people would pay to sit actually on the stage with the actors. The Globe Theatre was three storeys high and held about two thousand people. Gradually more and more money was spent on costumes, furniture and simple scenery, so that gradually acting and theatres became more like those of today.

1. Now answer the following questions from the passage:–

    a. Where and when was Shakespeare born?

    b. Whom did Shakespeare marry?

    c. Name two comedies and two tragedies written by Shakespeare.

    d. Why did acting stop in London for a while?

    e. Which famous theatre is associated with Shakespeare?

    f. Give two advantages of performing plays in the inn courtyards.

    g. Being part of an audience in those times was not very comfortable. Give two reasons for this.

    h. Who built the first permanent theatre? Where?

    i. Why did the plays have to be good?

    j. Where did the richer people sit in the theatre?

    k. What types of plays did the crowds enjoy?

    l. What general advancements were made in acting and theatre during this period? Refer closely to *all* the passage in answering this.

2. Write a couple of paragraphs explaining the main story of any of Shakespeare's plays that you may have read or heard of.

3. In TWELFTH NIGHT, Viola pretends to be her brother and becomes a boy servant to the Duke Orsino. When she realises she is in love with her master who still thinks she's a boy, complications arise. They are made worse when her twin brother Sebastian also turns up in the same place.

    In HAMLET, young Hamlet meets the ghost of his dead father who tells how he has been murdered and Hamlet vows to have his revenge on the murderer who has now married his mother.

    In ROMEO AND JULIET, a young boy and girl fall in love. Unfortunately, their two powerful families hate each other and would never allow them to meet·if they knew. Life is difficult enough for them but when Juliet is told that she is to marry another man her family has chosen for her, she and Romeo take desperate measures to stay together and the play ends in tragedy.

Above are three very simplified outlines of three of Shakespeare's plays. Do they sound good? Choose one of the ideas outlined above as the basis for a modern story or play. You may of course need to change the title and names of the characters.

The Designer

Most pupils aged 12–16 years enjoy this type of lesson and get great satisfaction from creating their own design work, but there may be some who need quite a bit of help and guidance and others who are unable to finish in the time allowed. Remember that pupils will need a variety of materials for this lesson e.g: cardboard, coloured pens, boxes, rubbers, fabric, glue, cellotape, safety pins and so on if they are to create anything worthwhile

1. Imagine you are one of a theatre's designers. You might be involved in lighting design, costume design or scenery/set design.

2. Now, depending upon your interests and what is actually available for you to use during this relatively short lesson, choose *one* of the following activities involving design work.

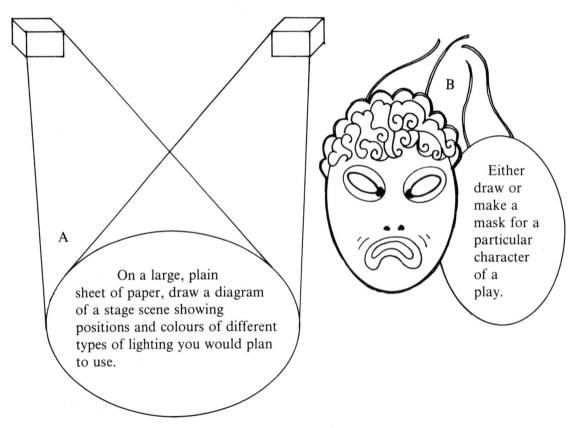

A On a large, plain sheet of paper, draw a diagram of a stage scene showing positions and colours of different types of lighting you would plan to use.

B Either draw or make a mask for a particular character of a play.

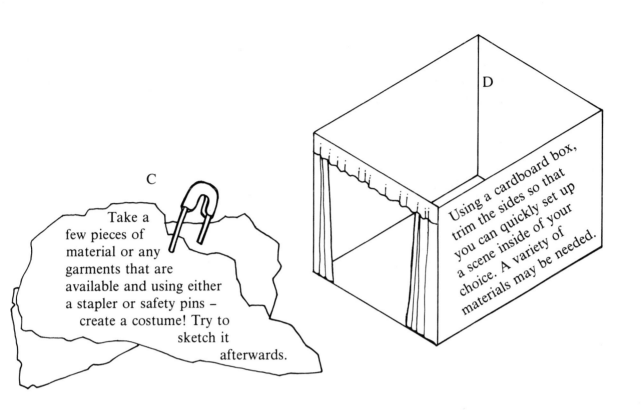

C

Take a few pieces of material or any garments that are available and using either a stapler or safety pins – create a costume! Try to sketch it afterwards.

D

Using a cardboard box, trim the sides so that you can quickly set up a scene inside of your choice. A variety of materials may be needed.

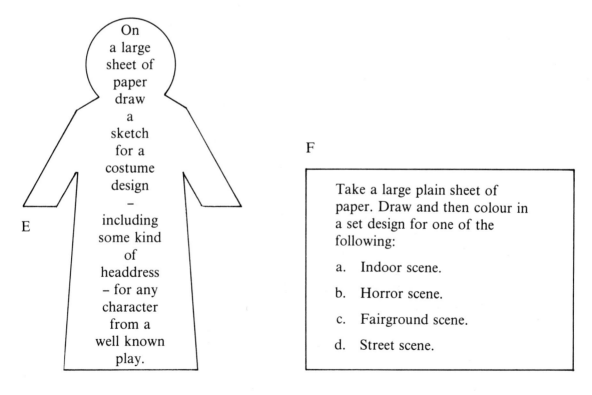

E

On a large sheet of paper draw a sketch for a costume design – including some kind of headdress – for any character from a well known play.

F

Take a large plain sheet of paper. Draw and then colour in a set design for one of the following:

a. Indoor scene.

b. Horror scene.

c. Fairground scene.

d. Street scene.

Using the Phone

This lesson teaches pupils to be more realistic when using the telephone in drama improvisations and is most suitable for pupils aged 11–13 years, although it can, of course, be used with other classes. It is sometimes advisable to read the information with the whole class before allowing them to begin the written work, for which they will need paper and pens.

1. Many drama improvisations include the use of the telephone. This may be an old one which is available as a prop or perhaps the telephone is mimed. In either case, the telephone calls are often very poorly acted out.

    There are many obvious mistakes; one is forgetting to dial the number when miming a telephone call – another is phoning someone whom you supposedly cannot see and yet you are looking directly at him or her throughout the telephone conversation that follows.

    However, what really ruins a group play is when the telephone is used quite incorrectly and therefore unrealistically. For instance; a tense, thoughtful piece of drama involving a serious accident is completely spoiled when someone runs to the telephone and shouts, "Help – my friend has been in an accident – come quickly!" and almost immediately afterwards the ambulance arrives! How did they know where they were? How did they decide to send an ambulance and not a fire engine?

    You should already know that in an emergency you need to dial 999. The operator then asks you which emergency service you require:– Police, Fire or Ambulance? Having been answered, you are put through to the appropriate switchboard. Another voice asks for some details such as who you are, what has happened and where you are. Only then can you expect help to arrive promptly. Similarly – a call to a large shop, business or even a school is not likely to be answered immediately by the very person you want to speak to. You must ask for that person first.

    Even if you are supposed to be just phoning a friend, you may need to wait for that person to be called to the phone before starting your conversation. Do remember, too, that the other person would probably interrupt you to speak themselves at times so you can't just say everything at once! You will obviously need to pause when imagining the other person is talking but do make sure the pause is long enough to have allowed them to speak! It might help to count to ten before pretending to reply in this case. But refer in your replies to what is said, so that the audience is kept informed.

    Of course, the telephone call can be used to create suspense or excitement in your play. Getting a wrong number by mis-dialling in a panic situation or having to wait a very long time before anyone answers or indeed no-one answering, all add to the dramatic effect of the moment.

    What happens if you are the one to answer the phone in a sketch or play? Well, all the above still applies of course but do remember too to give your number or name when you first pick up the receiver, and then immediately pause to allow the other person to say who they are and why they are phoning – before you start to talk.

Don't forget – telephone calls can add interest and realism to your drama work – but only if used properly!

2. Think carefully about different types of phone call and write out a suitable, realistic telephone conversation for each of the following situations.

A.

*An elderly woman has
been knocked over on
a busy main road.*

B.

*You wish to make a
complaint about
something or someone.*

C.

*You would like
information about a
house for sale or a
holiday.*

D.

*You want to make an
appointment with the doctor,
dentist or hairdressers or . . .*

E.

*You are phoning in
answer to an advertisement
for a job.*

F.

*You have just witnessed a
crime and are phoning the
police to report what
you've seen.*

G.

*You are phoning about an
interesting advertisement
you have seen in
the paper.*

H.

*Your child has gone
missing.*

General Theatre Quiz

(See page 45 for answers)

Pupils will need paper and pens and should work quietly on their own to answer this quiz. The questions are varied – some are easy, while others really test their knowledge of theatre or require them to turn to other sections of this book to look for answers. Therefore use either the whole quiz or part of it, with pupils aged 10–16 years, depending upon their ability.

1. Name any two places locally where you might expect to watch a play being acted.

2. What is acting without words called?

3. Name any two London theatres.

4. Name three famous actresses.

5. Name three famous actors.

6. Where was Shakespeare born? (If you are not sure look back at the Shakespeare section.)

7. Name three characters you might expect to find in a melodrama. (If you are not sure, look at the Victorian section.)

8. What is a script?

9. Name any city famous for its Mystery Cycle Plays. (If not sure, look back at the Medieval section.)

10. Name an actor who was famous for his parts in Silent Movie comedies.

11. Where would you go to try and get an actor's autograph after a performance?

12. Name three different categories of television programmes.

13. What strange 'stages' were used in Medieval times? (If not sure, look back at the Medieval section.)

14. Name any two of Shakespeare's plays. (If not sure, look back at the Shakespeare section.)

15. Name any two other famous plays.

16. Where would you buy your theatre tickets (in the theatre)?

17. Name two famous musicals.

18. Novels are divided into chapters; in what two ways are plays divided?

19. How did Greek actors help make themselves seen more clearly? (If not sure, look back at the Greek section.)

20. Name four different types of dancing.

21. Give the word meaning: a) a funny play; b) a sad play.

22. Which Pantomimes involve: a) a lamp? b) a cat? c) a goose? d) a pumpkin? e) two score robbers?

23. What do we call a person who helps tell the story in a play sometimes?

24. Write five lines describing any play you have watched in the theatre or on television recently.

ANSWERS TO THEATRE QUIZ (Marks out of 50)

1. For younger pupils accept the names of any two places where a play might reasonably be performed, e.g. schools, colleges, amateur drama group venues, youth theatres and so on as well as proper local theatres of course.

   Older pupils may only score 2 points if their answer includes at least one proper local theatre. (2 points)

2. Mime. (1 point)

3. Adelphi, Albery, Aldwych, Ambassadors, Apollo, Barbican, Comedy, Criterion, Dominion, Drury Lane, Theatre Royal, Duchess, Duke of York, Fortune, Garrick, Globe, Her Majesty's, Haymarket, Mermaid, Palace, Savoy, Shaftesbury, Shaw, St. Martins, Strand, Vaudeville, Victoria Palace, Westminster, Wyndhams, Young Vic, Phoenix, Piccadilly, Prince Edward, Prince of Wales, Queens, Royal Court, Old Vic, New London, National, London Palladium, Lyric Hammersmith, Lyric, Mayfair (2 points)

4. Teacher to award marks at own discretion. Do not accept singers, comedians, etc. (3 points)

5. Teacher to award marks at own discretion. Do not accept singers, comedians, etc. (3 points)

6. Stratford upon Avon. (1 point)

7. Wicked squire or equivalent, heroine/maiden in distress, awkward youth, hero. (3 points)

8. Written copy of the play read by actors in rehearsal. (1 point)

9. York, Chester, Coventry. (1 point)

10. Charlie Chaplin, Buston Keaton, Harry Lloyd. (1 point)

11. Stage Door. (1 point)

12. Documentary, comedy, plays, dramas, films, police or detective series, chat shows, quizzes, light entertainment, news. (3 points)

13. Carts. (1 point)

14. Merchant of Venice, Twelfth Night, Macbeth, Hamlet, Romeo and Juliet, As You Like It, All's Well that End's Well, The Taming of the Shrew, A Midsummer Night's Dream, King Lear, Othello, Antony and Cleopatra, Much Ado About Nothing, King John, Henry IV parts 1 & 2, Richard III etc. (2 points)

15. Teacher to use own discretion to award points. (2 points)

16. Box Office. (1 point)

17. Teacher to award marks accordingly. (2 points)

18. Acts and Scenes. (2 points)

19. Padded costumes, masks, platform shoes. (3 points)

20. Tap, Ballroom, Ballet, Modern, Robotics, Breakdancing, Disco, Folk, Latin American, etc. (4 points)

21. a) Comedy; b) Tragedy. (2 points)

22. Aladdin, Puss in Boots, Mother Goose, Cinderella, Ali Baba. (5 points)

23. Narrator. (1 point)

24. Teacher to mark according to clarity and content. (3 points)

Somewhere Different

Pupils should be able to work on their own in this lesson, which asks them to think about effective use of different settings in improvisation work. The lesson can be used with all pupils aged 9–16 years who will, of course, need paper and pens.

All too often young people are content to act out scenes set at home, at school, in the supermarket or at a football match. Try to get them to be more adventurous and original than that, by giving ideas for sketches set somewhere different.

1. Briefly write out 3 ideas for possible sketches for each of the following:–

    a. A jungle

    b. House of Commons

    c. The desert

    d. In Heaven

e. On a farm

f. At sea

g. On another planet

h. Northern Ireland

i. In prison

j. In an air raid/nuclear shelter

k. In the mountains

l. At a public execution

2. Now choose one of the ideas you thought of and write a more detailed account of how this could be used to create an interesting play. Mention plot, characters, time and any sound effects or lighting that might be needed. Or, you might have ideas for 'somewhere different' which is not already on the list.

3. Write a short play from one of the following titles: a. Trapped b. The Prize   c. If only . . .   d. The visitor

Decide first on the characters
                 the place – make it somewhere different
                 the problem – not an everyday one
                 the action
                 the ending

Remember that the characters must be very different from each other. Remember to give stage directions.

Remember that a play does not require speech marks and should be set out like this:–

JOHN: Here we are. This house is haunted you know (*he laughs*).
JANE: (*tearfully*) I'm scared!
JOHN: Oh, don't be such a baby. Come on. Let's go in.

(*more noises are heard*)

Stage and Screen Review

Questionnaires are so much more fun to do than most other kinds of written work. This one makes pupils aged 11–14 years really think about theatre and television, makes no demands upon the teacher and provides interesting material for future discussion work.

Try to answer each question as fully and honestly as you can.

1. How many hours do you spend watching television in an average day?

2. What sort of programmes do you most enjoy watching?

3. Name 3 well known TV actors or actresses.

4. Name your favourite television programme at the moment.

5. Explain why you like this programme so much.

6. Briefly describe any play you have seen on television in the last six months.

7. Name 6 different categories or types of television programmes.

8. Briefly describe any *two* characters from a soap opera or serial presently being shown on television.

9. Briefly list three advantages and three disadvantages of children watching television.

10. How often have you been to see a play performed on any stage (theatre, school, club, village hall) in the last year?

11. If you have watched many plays performed on stage – is this because you yourself are seriously interested in theatre or for some other reason?

12. If you have seldom or never watched a play performed on a proper stage – why is this?

13. Have you ever had the opportunity of looking around a theatre?

    Would this interest you?

14. Name 5 jobs to do with the theatre.

15. Name any play which has been performed locally in the last six months.

16. Have you ever been on a school trip to a theatre performance? Briefly desribe the play.

17. Would you be scared of going to the theatre without an adult present?

18. Name *four* types of performances you might see at the theatre.

19. Briefly describe any film you have watched recently.

20. Do you watch films on video or in the cinema – very often/fairly regularly/once in a while/rarely?

21. Who is your favourite film star? Explain why.

22. What type of film do you most enjoy watching? Why?

Lighting

All pupils aged approximately 14 – 16 years with a genuine interest in 'theatre' or who are taking a drama examination course will benefit form this work which is simple to do and requires the teacher to do no more then give out paper!

Read the following information on stage lighting and copy both this and the diagrams into your drama books or on to paper.

Lighting is important to any drama production. By careful use of stage lights you can change the mood from gloomy and sad to cheerful and bright; from cold, mysterious or sinister to warm, cosy and inviting. We can use stage lights to help change the scene or to let the audience know where the play is supposed to be set, without the inconvenience of lots of heavy scenery. Again, sunny daytime, evening half-light and shadowy night can all be represented by simply adjusting the stage lights or changing the colour filter.

There are many ways to light a stage or acting area, and many different kinds of lighting equipment are available to buy or hire, according to the needs of the group, theatre or individual production.

Spotlights

Spotlights work by the light of a 250–500 watt bulb being reflected forward to pass through a lens and become a beam of light which can then be focused. A strong metal casing helps to trap and direct this light and a colour filter can be placed in front of the spotlight to provide different shades and moods.

The Fresnel spotlight – This is used to provide a fixed, soft pool of light in which the actors can stand or move about. It allows main characters to be seen clearly or focuses upon an important grouping or scene. It can be used quite effectively on its own or with other spotlights to create several soft pools of light in different areas of the stage.

The Fresnel spotlight is often placed high up above the audience (Front of House) pointing down towards the stage or hung from the side gallery in much the same way. The angle of the beam and focusing can easily be adjusted for each production but cannot be altered during a performance.

The profile spotlight – This spotlight is very similar to the Fresnel spot but it produces a harder, clearer circle of light in a precise area or particular spot rather than a 'soft pool'. It can also be adjusted, the colour changed or it can be tilted in different directions as required throughout a performance. It therefore needs someone close to 'operate' it, although a large, modern theatre would use remote control. This spotlight can be positioned in the wings or facing the stage and is usually placed on a stand. It is the spotlight used to 'follow' an actor or compère about on stage.

Floodlights

A floodlight is a 150–250 watt bulb encased in a metal box. The light from the bulb is thrown forward by use of a large reflector behind it. There is no lens or other controls so it cannot be focused for example, but it can be tilted up or down slightly in preparation for a particular play. It cannot be adjusted during a performance. Larger floodlights that use a 500-watt bulb do exist, but generally floodlights are not as powerful as spotlights and just give a general lighting effect. Their purpose is to light the scenery and staging rather than the acting area and they can be hung individually or put together on a batten. They are placed high at the front of the stage on a bar normally but a batten can also be used at floor level on the front of the stage in which case they are called footlights. Different coloured filters can be placed in front of the lamps to produce a general mood or colouring for the set.

Lighting control

All the stage lights are connected into the lighting control unit. This may be a huge wall-mounted control box at the side of the stage or a compact portable unit. Whichever is the case all lighting can be controlled from this. By using dimmer levers you can dim the lights individually or all together, eventually achieving complete blackout. Or you can use the dimmers to bring up a new light slowly. You can alter the number of lights that are on at any one time and therefore get the exact effect you want on stage.

Colour filters

Colour filters are made from sheets of acetate. This can be bought as a roll and cut up as you wish to fit the various shapes and sizes of lights or bought as squares. There are many different colours available but the most popular are probably red, blue, green, yellow and pink. Once the sheet has been trimmed to the right size it fits into a colour frame which in turn is slotted into position just in front of the light casing. The acetate gets extremely hot and should not be touched by hand once in place. Care must also be taken that the acetate sheet is not placed too near the actual bulb as obviously this could cause a fire.

A whole range of other special lighting effects, too numerous to mention here, is also available from stage lighting companies. When you visit a theatre, try to get a look at the lighting control panel. Some panels look as complicated as the control panel of Concorde.

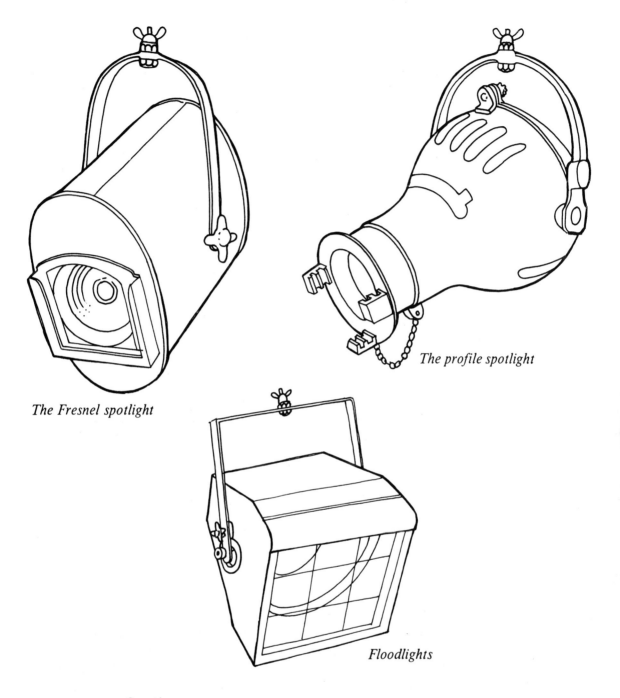

The Fresnel spotlight

The profile spotlight

Floodlights

Questions:

1. In what ways can lighting change a scene and the 'mood'?

2. Spotlights. How are they constructed? How does their use help the production?

3. What is the main purpose in using floodlights and footlights?

4. Why is the person in charge of the lighting control unit so very important?

Take a Proverb

This lesson helps pupils learn and understand proverbs as well as being a useful lesson for developing ideas for future improvisation work. It is suitable for all pupils aged 9–16 years although you may, of course, need to give some help to younger ones. Paper and pens are also needed.

1. Write down as many proverbs or well known sayings as you can think of. (15 might be average.)

    Here are 4 to get you started:–

    1. It's no use crying over spilt milk.

    2. Look after the pennies and the pounds will look after themselves.

    3. All work and no play makes Jack a dull boy.

    4. A stitch in time saves nine.

2. Now read through your list and check how many you really understand! (You may be able to ask the teacher for help with those you are unsure of.)

3. Choose five of these proverbs or well-known sayings and
    a. Write a few lines on each explaining its basic meaning.

    b. Write a few lines only on each showing how you could use it as the basis for an interesting sketch or play.

4. Choose any one idea from your work and now actually write a short play or sketch based on this. Your work should include a list of characters and possible scenes, and be at least one and a half sides long. You may or may not decide to use the proverb as the title.

Victorian Theatre

This simple lesson helps pupils to learn something of the history of drama, by reading the information on Victorian Theatre (including melodrama) and then completing the written work which follows. It is probably most suitable for pupils aged 13–16 years who will need paper and pens. You may or may not wish to read the passage with the whole class before allowing them to begin work on their own.

Before the Victorian age it was mostly the rich people who could afford to go to the small theatres to watch famous actors like David Garrick (1717–79) and Sarah Siddons (1775–1831) perform in well known plays like those of Shakespeare. Performances were held in the afternoon or as early as 5.00 p.m., when people would still be at work in the factories or shops.

During the Victorian period, however, both the theatres themselves and their audiences changed dramatically. London suddenly acquired a lot of theatres all competing with each other. Playbills and posters advertised their performances. Old theatres which had burnt down through using candles as lighting were rebuilt to hold larger audiences and to include better and changeable scenery, huge painted backcloths and different levels of staging. Lighting was now by gas-light. By burning a stick of lime in the gas jet one could direct a single soft beam on to one particular actor or part of the stage and later produce some special lighting effects. This was the beginning of modern stage lighting and explains the saying, 'being in the limelight'.

Shopkeepers, butchers and other tradesmen joined the queues for the cheapest seats in the theatres while, at the same time, many of the rich upper classes began to turn away from the theatre as opera, ballet, poetry and novels became more fashionable.

So, as the theatre became a more popular entertainment among the masses and audiences included the working classes as well as the wealthy, so the times of performances were also changed. The theatres would open at about 6.30 and performances would go on for many hours, including several different plays, so that workers who finished at, say, 8.00 p.m. could still go to the theatre to watch the second or third play of the evening.

The Victorian public wanted to be entertained with something spectacular, something with songs and plenty of action that roused their emotions without having to be 'thought' about. They also loved a happy ending.

The new 'melodramas' did exactly that. They told very simple stories usually involving a youthful hero, a damsel in distress and a wicked person of some kind. The acting was greatly exaggerated and needed little real skill. The plays were written in verse and gave plenty of scope for singing and dancing and lots of stage effects to produce the vivid spectacle the public wanted.

The earliest melodramas provided plenty of excitement, were set in exotic places and included ghosts and bandits. Later, melodramas were set in the country, in the present times, with a rustic hero and wicked squire. When one actor decided to play the character of a young sailor there was a sudden fashion for nautical melodramas and then later the dramatists turned to sensational crime stories such as Sweeney Todd and the murder of Maria Marten in the red barn as a basis for their plays. Even some of the popular Dickens novels were simplified and staged as crude melodramas.

The Victorian audience loved these lively melodramas. They could boo and hiss at the wicked villain, feel pity and concern for the poor maiden, laugh at the funny bits and finally rejoice in the happy ending. Melodramas continued to be the most popular theatre entertainment throughout the Victorian age and even today melodramas are still performed. Some are produced as examples of Victorian melodrama, while others are twentieth century versions, maybe no longer called by this title, but still using the same basic stories and flamboyant acting styles.

When the theatres decided eventually that the audiences might be getting bored with melodrama they began to produce plays that had a more interesting storyline and more thoughtful characters. Romances, comedies and a few serious plays were shown but these always included at least one sensational scene to satisfy the audiences' continued demand for 'spectacle'. Simplified versions of Shakespeare's plays were still being performed because of the very dramatic and spectacular scenes they often included.

One writer, Planche, created several fantasy extravaganzas including 'The Sleeping Beauty' and 'Beauty and the Beast' which used music, dancing and visual effects to the full. These were the forerunners of our modern pantomimes and for the first time an actress played the leading man.

Other dramatists of this time wanted to produce more realistic plays. Drawing room scenes were designed, using a lot of real furniture with several stage flats joined together and decorated to create walls, thus making the whole scene look as real as possible. The introduction of electric lighting in theatres at this time also helped considerably. Costuming was also given more thought.

Despite all these new plays, however, melodramas remained unchallenged as the most popular Victorian entertainment until the introduction of the 'Music Hall' in the latter half of the century.

The Music Hall became the place where the working classes could go to relax after a hard day's work. Here they could sit and drink while being entertained by a variety of popular acts.

With the rougher elements of their audiences being removed to the Music Halls, the theatres hoped that the upper classes would return to the theatre and plays would become respectable again. Smaller theatres were now built and the evening's performance was reduced to one 'good' play. The introduction of little changes, like a detailed programme instead of a cut down playbill, providing a matinee performance which meant only those not working could attend, and serving tea or coffee during the interval, helped persuade the polite society to return.

The new Gilbert and Sullivan operas proved especially popular with these new audiences and more refined social comedies and dramas were now shown. Henry Irving was the first to decide that the auditorium should be in darkness so that all lighting could be concentrated on the stage. General acting standards also improved.

The theatre gradually became not only respectable again but also fashionable. The witty plays of Oscar Wilde brought the very best of society circles back into the theatres and seats were now booked in advance. The advance of the railways also meant that famous actors and actresses could take the well-known London plays on a tour of smaller towns.

Playwrights began to have their plays printed so that the more intellectual could read them as well as see them performed. One famous playwright called George Bernard Shaw wanted his plays to contain a message. He wrote about poor people living in slums and generally showed up the evils of his time. Although such controversial content meant that many of his plays were at first banned from the stage, those who read copies of his plays began to realise the truth of what he wrote and finally persuaded theatres to show them. Although they contained a serious message, Shaw's plays were also written in an interesting way and were often amusing to watch. So, by the time of his death, George Bernard Shaw had become famous. Other serious plays were being produced as well as the polite society dramas and comedies.

The Victorian theatre, therefore, presented us with much of the theatre we know today. Theatre lighting was established, scenery and staging was much improved, new plays were written in a variety of styles – many still being performed today – and theatre had extended to towns outside London. Many of the original Victorian theatres still remain, particularly in London, where their names remind us of famous Victorian theatre people. Music Halls, too, continued to provide entertainment for the working classes for a long time after the end of the Victorian age.

1. Use the information about Victorian theatre to answer the following questions:

    a. What changes were made in stage lighting during the Victorian times?

    b. What type of play proved the most popular in Victorian theatres? Why was it so popular?

    c. What made the working classes move away from the theatres towards the end of the century?

    d. Name any two things that helped bring the upper classes back into the theatres.

    e. Why were Shaw's plays at first banned on the London stage?

2. Using the above passage as a guide, write out your own account of Victorian theatre. About 150 words.

Making Sounds

This lesson, which is most suitable for pupils aged 9–13 years, uses sounds rather than speech to show younger pupils how important expression and tone of voice is to meaningful acting. It could, however, be used quite successfully with older pupils, by omitting the first section and allowing more time on the final scenes.

INTRODUCTION (to be read to the class):

    a. *Work on your own, acting out all the activities to do with getting up in the morning and eventually leaving for school. You must make all the sounds that go with the actions: e.g. the alarm going off, waking up slowly, turning on the taps and washing, eating breakfast and so on.*

    b. *Now think about the sounds you are making. Do they sound realistic? It should be obvious from your sounds whether breakfast consists of toast, egg and bacon, cereals or porridge for instance and any conversation with imaginary other people should be easily understood even though actual words are not used.*

1.   Get into pairs and quickly act out the following very short scenes using 'sounds' rather than speech just as you did before.

    a.   Headmaster telling off a pupil who begins by answering back but ends up crying perhaps.

    b.   One of you is about to commit suicide by jumping off the window ledge; the other is trying to talk you out of it.

    c.   One is serving in the chip shop; the other is returning to complain about the burnt chips.

    d.   You are giggling and talking about somebody who walks past or is sitting nearby.

2.   If there is time, you might like to show your work to the rest of the class.

3.   Finally, get into groups if you wish, or remain as pairs, and work out any short scenes where you make the sounds of everything that goes on as well as acting it. An office scene, train, football match or hairdresser's are usually the easiest to do although, of course, any scene could be chosen.

4.   Show one of these scenes to the rest of the class.

Choose a Title

A very simple lesson for any teacher to supervise and one which allows pupils to use their imaginations to the full. This lesson is ideally suited to any pupils aged between 9–16 years.

1.   Choose one of the titles shown below.

    a.   Stuck.

    b.   Memories.

    c.   The visitor.

d. The experiment.

e. The phone call.

2. Working in a pair or a group, make up an interesting improvisation based on the title you have chosen. You may decide to use the whole lesson for this, if you have a particularly good idea which needs to be properly developed and carefully acted out.

3. If, however, the last improvisation was a short one and you therefore have time left, choose another title from the list above and work out a second improvisation from that. Try to develop your ideas a little more fully this time.

4. Show your work, if you wish, to the rest of the class.

Foreign Parts

Pupils usually enjoy this, which often produces some amusing and original work. Although most suitable for pupils aged 11–14 years, it can be used quite successfully with both younger and older pupils.

1. Working in a pair or threesome, allow yourself five or ten minutes only to act out short sketches based on the following situations.

    a. You are a couple looking through holiday brochures, slowly realising that you each have a very different idea of what makes a perfect holiday.

    b. Something goes wrong at customs or when you arrive abroad.

    c. You are trying, with extreme difficulty, to make a foreigner understand you.

2. Either in a group or remaining as a pair – think more carefully about different aspects, or interpretations, of the title 'Foreign Parts', e.g. ski-ing accident, smuggling, scene at the travel agent's, foreign piece of machinery, rowing up the river in the jungle, stationed abroad during the war and so on.

3. Work out an interesting, and possibly amusing, improvisation from one of your ideas. Show this to the rest of the class when you have finished if there is time.

Mime

Most suitable for pupils aged 9–12 years, this short lesson on mime is simple for both teacher and pupils and should be taken as a starting point for a whole range of possible mime work using poetry, music and more sophisticated situations.

1. *Introduction*: Sit the class in a circle, preferably on the floor. Mime various objects being passed around such as a large hat, pinch of salt, sticky, half-eaten toffee, bag of crisps, feather, rabbit, milkbottle. Make comments about the items, have fun trying on the hat or stroking the rabbit. Have two items being passed around at the same time so that waiting does not lead to lack of concentration. Make sure that even small details are observed.

2. Now that they have the idea of miming objects, keep to the circle but introduce a ball. Decide what sort of ball it is and start throwing it from one person to another. After a while change the type and size of the ball and get them to adjust their miming in the throwing game. Keep changing the ball – eventually it may even be a marble that needs to be rolled. If the pupils really concentrate and the mime is effective it will seem as if there really is a ball being thrown and caught and pupils will leave the circle to fetch it if they didn't manage to catch it.

3. Get pupils to mime the following situations on their own in a space.

   a. Waiting at the bus stop in the pouring rain.

   b. Preparing for an important visitor.

   c. Being tired in an office where the phone keeps ringing, the desk drawer sticks and the paperwork presents a problem. (Remark upon different people's mannerisms here.)

4. In pairs: mime a scene at the hairdresser's, starting from just before the entrance of a customer. Remember details like the towel over the shoulders; does the shampoo come from a bottle, sachet or tube. Where is the basin? (They nearly always stand in it!) Is the hair dryer ever switched on? And so on.

5. Stop the class after a few minutes only. Allow one half of the class to sit down and watch the other half, then swop over. Ask for criticisms and comments while they watch.

6. If there is *still* time left, the pairs can begin miming other simple situations

such as burglars, having a good meal in a restaurant then discovering they have no money, or scenes in a park.

Stage Set

Suitable for all pupils aged 9 – 16 years. This lesson is ideal if you have a drama studio and plenty of stage blocks etc., but can still be worked fairly efficiently with just a few chairs and perhaps a desk. You will need to set up an arrangement of furniture in the middle of the room for pupils to use as the stimulus for their improvisation work. This might involve lots of chairs and tables (possibly upturned) to suggest a complicated scene or it could be simply two chairs and a desk in the background. Remember, it is the pupils' imaginations that are required so don't be too fussy or take too much time over this. It is surprising how imaginative they can be in this lesson!

1. Get into a group of any number and sit together in a space.

2. Now look at the 'set' that has been arranged in the middle of the room for you. This may be a very simple one of perhaps just a chair and a table or may suggest a more complicated scene.

3. Within your group, discuss ideas as to how you could use this 'set' to create an imaginative and interesting improvisation or sketch. You may not alter the 'set' in any way and, of course, you cannot use it to practise on.

4. After a few minutes to think, and possibly practise, show your improvisation or sketch to the rest of the class, using the 'set' in whichever way you have decided.

5. When all (or some) of the classes' improvisations have been shown, take turns in your groups to arrange a new 'set' to be used.

Odd Words

All pupils aged 9 – 16 years can produce interesting drama work using this slightly unusual method of picking out odd words to be somehow used in an imaginative and original group improvisation. You will, of course, need to provide quite a lot of small slips of paper which may be written on in advance or given to the pupils to do. The warm-up is a popular one, easy to organise and quite effective with even an otherwise lethargic group.

1. QUICK WARM UP:– Everyone stands in a space while the teacher or one pupil explains the meaning of various colours: red = freeze, green = travel around the room, amber = sit down, white = get into pairs, black = get into threes.

2. Starting obviously with green, everyone travels around the room. The teacher or a chosen pupil calls out different colours and the rest must quickly obey the order that is associated with that colour. The last one to respond to the colour called, plus anyone who responds with the wrong action is immediately eliminated. Continue calling colours and eliminating pupils until only one person, the winner, is left. Quick and clever calling should ensure that this warm up only lasts 3 or 4 minutes.

3. New colours and different speeds of travelling for green can obviously be introduced later. As well as physically preparing you for active improvisation, the emphasis of this warm up is on quick thinking – which is needed for the following activity.

4. IMPROVISATION WORK:– You will need a lot of small slips of paper with one word written on each. One of the students (or the teacher) can either prepare these in advance or give a slip to each one in the class and get them to write down a word at random. If the class does the slips you will need to collect them in and mix them up quickly. Fold all the slips and place them in some kind of container.

5. Arrange yourselves into groups of four. Each person of each group then picks out one slip of paper and takes it back to his group. Therefore, each group now has four slips and four different words in its possession.

6. Each group has to now improvise a scene in which all the words are used, or based upon the four words in some way. Allow yourself only a few minutes for this.

7. Show any sketches which seem interesting.

Statues

Pupils aged 9– 13 years will particularly enjoy this lesson as it gives them the opportunity for simple comedy work, but of course it can be used with older groups too.

1. In pairs act out the following scenes very briefly.

a. 2 old people stop to rest on a park bench.

b. 2 spies meet secretly at a statue in park.

c. Couple stopping to look in a shop window.

d. 'Know-it-all' intellectual showing someone around the museum.

e. Either two people who have been drinking or one drunkard and another character in park or High Street.

2. Either remain in your pair or make up a slightly larger group and consider the following situation which could be set anywhere where there are statues or dummies, e.g. Madame Tussaud's, Art Gallery, shop window, park, etc.

   Situation: One, or more, of the group is convinced, rightly or wrongly, that one of the statues/dummies has moved.

   Think carefully about your characters and their individual reactions, your setting and the time.

3. Work out a sketch from your ideas. It *may* be a serious sketch although the situation probably lends itself more easily to comedy work.

The Problem

This 'social drama' lesson is an important one as it helps pupils understand and deal with problems that affect themselves or others in an enjoyable way. It is suitable for use with pupils aged 12–16 years and can be easily taught by a non-specialist teacher.

Dear Jane,

Please can you help? I'm always in trouble at school, I don't understand half the work and the teachers all pick on me. Sometimes the other kids pick on me too and threaten to beat me up if I don't do what they say. I can't tell anyone 'cos they wouldn't believe me.

Dear Jane,

My problem is my parents. They really show me up and embarrass me all the time! They still treat me like a four year old. I'm not allowed out late and I have to wear really awful clothes! What can I do?

1. Set out above are two letters which might be found on the problem page of a teenage magazine. They describe fairly common teenage problems but of course there are many, many more and it's not just teenagers who have problems. Everyone has problems of some kind, whether they are really

serious ones or just problems like catching the wrong train or losing their false teeth!

2. In a group of three or four, make a quick list of ten different problems that people might have. Do not include any of those already mentioned here.

3. When you have done this, look back through your list and discuss some of them. Decide upon one problem which you think would be easy and interesting to act out in your group. Remember, your sketch need not necessarily be a very serious one.

4. Spend about ten minutes practising your sketch and then show it to the rest of the class if there is time.

Imagination Stretchers

Use this lesson almost as a game with any class of pupils aged 9–16 years. It will really make them think about all the different ways a word or title can be interpreted and might help them avoid always using the most obvious ideas in future improvisations or in the examination. Some rough paper may be needed for writing lists.

1. Divide the class into groups of four or five. Each group should be equal in number and ability as far as possible.

2. Give a title and ask each group to compile a list of different ways in which this title could be interpreted . . . e.g. Lost = a) lost your way; b) lost key; c) lost memory; d) lost a friend; e) lost chance etc etc.

3. Encourage competition between groups. Either give a time in which list is to be completed (1/2 minutes) or stop when first group succeeds in reaching certain number (10/15).

4. Decide which group has 'won' then read out and discuss all the possible interpretations, particularly those which would make interesting improvisations.

5. Give a new title and start again. This can be repeated several times to awaken their imaginations and get some really good ideas. Pupils usually enjoy the idea of competing in this way and the activity becomes fun as well as useful.

POSSIBLE TITLES: Parting, Lost, Memories, Number Ten, Meeting, Chance.

6. *Possible follow up work*: Ask each group to choose any one idea which has resulted from these imagination stretchers and use it as the basis of an improvised sketch.

One Word Story Plays

This fairly difficult method for creating improvisation work is probably most suitable for those pupils aged 14–16 years and requires some initial guidance from the teacher.

1. Get into groups of between 4–6. Start making up a story but with each member of the group only allowed to contribute one word at a time.

   e.g. 1. One

   2. Saturday

   3. I

   4. was

   5. feeling

   6. bored

   1. so

   2. I

   3. went

   4. to

   5. see ....and so on until you have finished the story.

2. This is quite difficult and each member should think before saying his or her word so that the story has a chance to develop into an interesting one.

3. Once you have mastered this storytelling technique, start on a new 'one word story' but this time stop once it begins to get interesting and start acting instead. In other words – when you've created an interesting idea – use it as the basis for a play.

4. Complete your play remembering to return to the 'one word story' method if your ideas dry up again.

Persuasion

Pupils aged 9–16 years should enjoy acting out these simple and often amusing sketches which concentrate on speech work.

This lesson will help you gain confidence and improve your speech work in drama.

1. Get into pairs and act out:

    a. Trying to persuade your mum or dad to let you do something you know they'll be against.

    b. Trying to persuade a friend to do something for you.

2. Still in pairs or threes: work out a very short sketch where one of you is a salesman trying to sell some completely useless item to the other(s), e.g: a book which has the same thing written on every page, a pair of shoes with no soles, a washing up bowl with holes in it. The other person(s) may or may not be persuaded to buy this object.

3. Using any of the ideas given in (1) or (2) – perhaps creating a new situation of your own – act out a slightly longer and more complicated sketch where someone has to persuade someone else in some way but make it as difficult as possible for the 'persuader' to succeed.

4. Show your work to the rest of the class if there is time.

Strange Phrases – Improvisation Game

Try this unusual but interesting game with classes aged approximately 12–15 years. It is sensible to have a few suitably odd phrases written down before the lesson begins so that a) you don't get stuck for ideas halfway through and b) you can give these to one of the pupils and allow her/him to be chairman.

Some suggestions are 'I do like your wetsuit'/'Follow that bus'/'The Queen's coming to tea'/'My wellies are stuck'/'We shall have to move the cabbages'.

1. The class divides into two teams A + B. Either the teacher or 1/2 pupils is chosen to be in charge, to give out phrases and award the points throughout.

2. 2 pupils from Team A go to this person and are secretly given a scene or situation to act briefly and a rather strange phrase that they must include at some point during their sketch, e.g. Hospital scene – 'pass the carrots over'. The person in charge will need to think of a lot of different scenes and phrases!

3. *After no more than a minute* to think, these 2 pupils return and act out their sketch, being careful to include the strange phrase in such a way that it casually blends into the situation and does not make it too obvious for Team B, who have to guess what the phrase was.

4. Team B is allowed 2 guesses. If they guess correctly straight away they are awarded 2 points. If they guess correctly on their second go they are awarded 1 point only. If they guess incorrectly both times then the players' team have one chance to guess correctly for one bonus point.

5. 2 pupils from Team B then come up, get a phrase and act out their sketch for Team A to guess, and so on.

6. The game continues until everyone has had a chance to act or the bell goes!

Thief, Drunkard, Liar!

Although this 'social drama' lesson can be used with all pupils aged 11–16 years, you will probably find the most perceptive and interesting work comes from those aged 14–16 years.

1. Working with a partner show a scene in which one of you steals something from either a house, shop, school or friend. It may be something important or quite trivial, as you wish. The second person may be a suspicious or concerned friend; an alert or dozy shopkeeper; or perhaps a parent who finds out. Remember the reaction and character of the second person needs to be as convincing as the first.

2. Now, either in your pair again or in a group, act out a scene in which one of you discovers something not quite 'nice' about a person you thought you knew well. This could be anything from realising your mum is an alcoholic or your dad is a criminal, to finding out your friend is on drugs or your girl/boyfriend has told you a pack of lies. Think carefully and honestly about what you really would do in this type of situation and try to keep your acting and chosen scenes as realistic and convincing as possible.

3. If there is time, you may like to show your ideas to the rest of the class.

Puppets

This fun way of developing movement and speech skills is best used with pupils aged 9–13 years, who may need a little guidance. However, older pupils too might sometimes enjoy trying the second part!

Ask the class to get into pairs.
One pupil needs to be higher than the other, so they must use a chair or table to stand on or else stand behind a chair with the partner sitting down.

2.   The person who is higher is the puppeteer pulling imaginary strings connected to the head and limbs of the other person, the puppet. They must devise an interesting and fairly complicated puppet sequence between them.

3.   The pairs then change places and work out a new human puppet sequence. Perhaps even join with another pair so there are now two puppets to form an interesting sketch.

4.   Now for something slightly different: collect together one or two objects – a jumper, shoe or schoolbag will do if nothing else is available. In pairs they must try to describe, demonstrate, sell or even tell a story about one of these objects, with one being the hands and arms and the other being the voice! To do this:– one stands behind the other. The person in front is the voice and places his or her arms folded behind his or her back. The person behind stands close enough to reach and hold the objects with his or her arms and makes it look as if the arms actually belong to the person in front. Even when they have got the positioning right, it isn't easy to co-ordinate each others' voice and hand movements!

5.   Get them to change places and try a different object or even try acting out a more complicated routine in this way.

Myths and Legends

Many myths and legends make excellent 'starters' for improvisation work and pupils benefit from learning more about these ancient tales in this simple lesson for pupils aged 10–14 years.

1.   *In pairs try this drama exercise*: You must hold a conversation for two minutes without stopping, but neither of you may say 'yes' 'no' or 'I' at all during the conversation. Each time you make a mistake a part of your body becomes frozen: head, body, arms, legs. The person who becomes totally frozen first is the loser and the other partner wins.

2.   *Quickly discuss* this famous Greek myth of King Midas. He was an extremely greedy man who thought he had done well when his wish for everything he touched to turn to gold was granted. Unfortunately this included his food, drink and even his daughter, which left poor Midas far

from happy. The gods eventually felt sorry for him and turned everything back to normal but gave Midas donkey's ears to remind him of his foolishness and greed.

3. *Work out* a quick sketch to show this story.

4. *There are many other famous myths*, legends and old tales which could easily be turned into good drama sketches. For example: the Legend of Robin Hood, The Loch Ness Monster, and King Arthur. Lots of local tales of haunted houses or headless horsemen could all be used to create interesting drama work. Try to think of other old tales, myths or legends that you know or have heard of.

5. *Or, if you'd like to try another* ancient Greek Myth: what about these stories of 'Orpheus' or 'Narcissus and the Echo':-

   a. Orpheus was so upset when his wife, Eurydice, got bitten by a snake and died, that he decided he would go to the underworld, the land of the dead, to try and get her back. He was a wonderful musician and so used his music to charm his way past all the terrible guards and then to try to persuade the powerful and cold Hades, God of the underworld, to release her. Hades eventually agreed to allow Eurydice to return, with Orpheus, back to the land of the living on one condition. Eurydice would follow behind Orpheus but if he once looked back at her, before safely reaching home, she would disappear for ever. Orpheus left the underworld and kept his promise, until the very last moment when he was so worried in case she was not there that he could no longer resist the temptation to look back and check. Sadly, as Orpheus quickly glanced back so Eurydice began to fade slowly away and disappear for ever.

   b. The story of Narcissus and Echo may give you several ideas for funny or serious drama improvisations:- Zeus, King of all the Greek Gods, was in a good mood when he visited earth one afternoon and heard Echo's beautiful voice as she sang to the children. He gave them all a golden apple from his wife's special tree, as a treat, and then returned to the home of the Gods above. Hera, his wife, was furious when she learnt of his generosity with her apples and as she was a very jealous Goddess she decided to take revenge on poor Echo, by taking away her beautiful voice. Echo could not speak or sing – all she could do was repeat the last words of anything anyone said to her.
   Meanwhile, Narcissus was lost in the woods. He was an extremely attractive young man and he knew it! He was so vain he was always telling himself how beautiful he was and how he could never love anyone who was not as beautiful as himself. He met Echo and asked her the way out of the woods. She instantly fell in love with

him but he thought her stupid because she just kept repeating his words. Echo was so upset she asked her Goddess friend Venus to make her disappear, and only her voice remained – as an echo.

Narcissus by now had sat down by the river. He looked into the water and saw the most beautiful face ever seen. He spoke to the face and heard an echo of his voice. Believing it to be some beautiful water nymph and not realising he was in love with his own reflection, he stayed on the riverbank forever, staring into the water at the lovely face. Eventually he took root in the bank and turned into the flower we now call 'Narcissus'.

6. *Use any myth, legend* or old tale you can think of or have read here as the basis for a short improvisation – working either in pairs or small groups.

7. *You may wish* to show your work if there is time available.

Improvisation from Titles

This simple lesson which can be taken by any teacher, allows pupils of any age or ability between 9 – 16 years complete freedom to choose a title and work in groups to create their own interesting play or improvisation.

1. Look at the titles given below. In pairs or groups of four – choose any one title that seems interesting and work out an improvisation in some way connected to that title.

   1. The Mistake

   2. Voices in the dark

   3. The Secret

   4. Help!

2. If you have worked hard during the lesson to produce an interesting and well acted improvisation, you may wish to show it to the rest of your class.

Odd Shoes

All pupils aged 9 – 16 years will have fun acting out the comedy sketches contained in this lesson while you, the teacher, need do little more than watch and enjoy their finished work.

The following ideas for improvisation give plenty of scope for comedy work. Think carefully about facial expression, movement and speech throughout, as these will help your comedy to be more successful.

1. *In pairs* – act out this situation: One of you is very late meeting a friend in a public place. The friend has been getting more and more fed up with waiting and demands to know the reason for your delay. Then, at some point in your conversation or following actions, the friend notices you are wearing odd shoes! He/she may or may not decide to tell you about this. What happens next is up to you; and remember, the shoes may be as 'odd' as you wish.

2. Either: a) Act out a similar situation where one of you is somehow dressed in a strange way. It may be a mistake which you or your friend notice too late or there may be a reason for it.

   b) Act out a restaurant scene where one of you realises you have left your money at home – only after you've eaten your expensive meal.

3. If there is still time, develop your scenes further or show one of your sketches to the rest of the class.

'Freeze!'

This is a way of getting pupils to improvise in pairs in a short time, which is both great fun and encourages quick thinking and confidence. It is suitable for all pupils aged 9–16 years although older pupils will obviously produce the best work. You will need to explain what happens quite carefully before you begin to avoid possible confusion or embarrassment later. Although some pupils may be reluctant at first, confident and able pupils can produce some very quick, imaginative and often hilarious changes of scene, characters and so on. And there is never a shortage of pupils wanting to shout 'Freeze!' and catch them in an amusing or awkward position.

1. Pupils sit in a large circle. Choose two people to stand in the middle. Somebody else in the class then gives them a mime each . . . e.g: Sarah is preparing dinner; John is a milkman on his rounds.

2. Choose another person who is going to shout 'Freeze!'

3. Having been given their individual mimes, the two in the middle of the circle start acting. After a couple of minutes, or when he feels it could be interesting, the chosen pupil shouts 'Freeze!' and they must do exactly that. Then, carefully considering the position in which they have frozen

but reacting as quickly as possible, the quickest thinking one of the pair starts to improvise a sketch suggested to him by his frozen position and the other one joins in with this. After a minute or so 'Freeze!' is shouted again and they change to a new sketch suggested by one of their frozen positions.

4. This is repeated two or three times and then a new pair is chosen, given mimes, etc.

Over the Wall

This easy lesson can be used successfully with pupils of any ability aged between 9–16 years. Obviously, younger pupils will tend to create rather simple sketches while older pupils should be able to produce some quite thoughtful and original acting. Remember you will need to set up a 'wall' in front of the class – perhaps by using 3 chairs placed together – for them to use when they show their work. Although some groups are rather inhibited and find it difficult to do section (4), this can be an ideal way of assessing the ability and confidence of a new group and might even be used at the beginning of the lesson rather than at the end, for this purpose.

1. In pairs – work out a short sketch that involves a wall, fence or hedge in any way you wish. This could be simply two neighbours talking over the garden fence or burglars trying to get into the grounds of a large house, or you may have a better idea of your own. If there are chairs or other furniture available you might be able to use these as your fence, wall or hedge.

2. As soon as you've had a chance to practise your sketch, get a chair and sit with the rest of the class facing the 'wall'.

3. Show your short sketch to the rest of the class by using this wall, fence or hedge. Remember to face them as much as possible when acting and speak up so everyone can hear you. You will, of course, be able to watch the other sketches too.

4. Now, without leaving the semi-circle this time, try to think up new ideas for an interesting scene that uses this wall, fence or hedge in some way. Be as imaginative and original as you can, and when you think you have a good idea, go up *immediately* either in a pair or on your own and act out your new sketch in front of the class.

Play for Today

Older pupils (especially the 14–16 age group) enjoy this type of social drama and often produce the most interesting and realistic work. Each group may need rough paper for listing problems in (1) but otherwise they should be able to work with little or no assistance.

1. There are many problems facing people living in today's world: racial prejudice, starvation, conflict in families, glue sniffing, wars and football vandalism are just a few of the problems encountered by modern society in various countries.

    In a group – make a list of 20 or more such problems and discuss how each might be suitable or effective as the basis of a 'Play for Today'.

2. In groups – choose one of your ideas from above and work out a really thoughtful play. Several linked scenes will help build up an understanding of main characters and give greater insight into the important topic you have chosen. Remember to keep all acting realistic and decide upon the best style of presentation for your play. Is it to be satirical (comedy with an underlying serious note) or presented as a kind of documentary or given as one person's life story?

3. Using scenery and props, if they are available, may help you make the play seem more convincing, but remember that clarity of ideas and good acting are the most important factors. So take time over this.

Looking Down

You will probably need to supervise the warm-up exercise and give some help to younger pupils in their improvisation work but generally this is an easy lesson to teach and is suitable for all pupils aged 11–16 years.

1. *Warm up*: Everyone stands in a space. Choose a class leader (or the teacher) to give some simple moves and exercises so that you become more in the mood for acting after perhaps a long lesson huddled over a desk. Try to ensure that all parts of your body are used in this general limbering up. Perhaps two or three of you might take turns to be the leader.

2. *Improvisation*: Get into a group of three and improvise the following scenes. You are allowed only a few minutes for each.

    a. One of you is an angel looking down on earth. You have been given the task of trying to change one of the other two into a better person . . .

b. A man/woman looks back from Heaven and sees how he/she died. Perhaps they could have avoided this? Or do they now want revenge on someone in some way?

3. Show any good improvisations which have resulted.

4. In your group discuss other ideas and interpretations of the title 'looking down'.

5. Now arrange yourselves into perhaps larger groups and using any ideas you have thought of from the title, or expanding on ideas in 2, you have a longer time in which to work out a new, more interesting and thoughtful improvisation.

6. Show your finished work if there is time.

Trapped

This improvisation work is suitable for all pupils aged 11 – 16 years and could be used as an introduction to 'serious drama'. Some rough paper may be needed for 2.

1. *In Pairs* – briefly act out the following scenes:

   a. One of you gets your foot/arm or head trapped in something. The other person is trying to help release you.

   b. You find yourselves somehow trapped in a lift, rotating door or room.

   c. One of you pleads with a parent to be allowed out in the evening but for some reason the answer is firmly 'no' and so you feel trapped indoors.

2. Think carefully about the title 'Trapped'. This title can form the basis for many different stories and can be used in a variety of different ways whether comedy or tense drama. Get a piece of paper and either in a pair or group make a list of six different ways you could use 'Trapped' as a title for an improvisation.

3. Now choose one of the ideas from your list and use it as the basis for an interesting and fairly long improvisation or sketch to be completed and possibly shown by the end of the lesson.

Cheese Fugue

Although most suitable for pupils aged 10–13 years, you may find one or two older groups enjoy this rather unusual exercise, too. Be prepared to give groups quite a bit of help to begin with as they might be slightly hesitant. However, once they really get started, pupils often have great fun creating their 'fugues' and produce some imaginative and original work.

This is a somewhat unusual lesson and you may find you are a little hesitant at first but once your group starts to develop the fugue you will probably find it's great fun and some very interesting and amusing work can be produced. This lesson helps you to be more aware of rhythm, movement and sound, and the same technique can be used again and again to enhance your work in other areas of improvisation. The theme of cheeses has been chosen to explain this but you may use the same method for virtually any group of things: e.g. – different meats, flowers, school subjects, colours and so on.

1. Get into groups of between 4 and 6 and think of as many names of different cheeses as possible. Here are some to help you: Stilton, Danish Blue, Processed, Camembert, Gouda, Edam, Red Leicester, Gloucester, Parmesan, Caerphilly, Philadelphia; don't forget there are many more. You may want to write the list down. Then discuss the various ways in which these could be said. E D A M may be said in a squeaky voice, for instance. G O R G O N Z O L A may suggest a deep and foreign sounding voice while another may be spoken with a country/farm type accent. (If you have chosen meats as your theme then one may be sausages, another lamb, another chicken, another hamburger, and so on in the same way.)

2. Now, each person in the group chooses a different cheese (or meat, subject, drink, etc) and decides how he or she is going to say it. Make sure that the cheeses chosen give plenty of variation within your group.

3. Each group now makes up a kind of rhythm or song using their cheeses, (or meats, flowers, drinks, etc.), e.g. Cheddar cheddar cheddar, gor . . . gon . . . zola. Cheddar cheddar cheddar, edam! . . . Red Leicester – cheddar . . . Red Leicester – cheddar . . . edam! edam! . . . processed cheese! This will probably take quite a while to work out. Notice the cheeses need to be said at different speeds as well and some cheeses will be said more often than others.

4. Having given the cheeses different characters and speeds to make the song, now give each cheese a movement to go with the character. In this way, your group can create anything from a dance-drama to a machine or dance routine or funny advert. You should be as imaginative as possible and think of an effective start and finish to your fugue.

5. Show your finished work.

Set a Scene

This is a delightful lesson which pupils aged 11 – 16 years always enjoy and which makes little demand upon the teacher. After the initial organisation, the pupils set the scene, the characters and improvise situations with little or no help from you. Some rough paper should be available for their planning.

1. Get into pairs or threes. You will need a sheet of paper and a pencil between you.

2. Now quickly draw a rough diagram of a large place such as a hospital, airport, large shop or zoo, showing all the different parts of the place, e.g. office, canteen, operating theatre, sweet counter, customs control and so on. Look at the diagram below if you are not sure how to do this.

3. Now count up the number of people present in your class and subtract 2 or 3. This tells you how many people or 'characters' you can use in your diagram. Use an X to show where each character is to be placed in this building or area you've drawn.

FOR EXAMPLE: HOSPITAL SCENE = 24 CHARACTERS

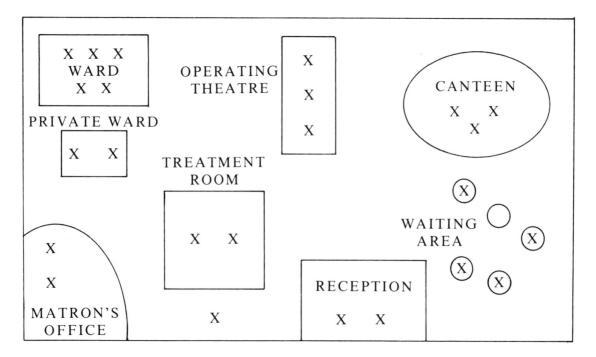

4. Ask your teacher to choose one pair or threesome to be the scene-setter-directors while the rest of you line up at one end of the room. Whoever is chosen then sets up the scene they have just drawn by placing the rest of you, in turn, in different areas of the drama hall and telling you what character you are supposed to be, and giving you some idea of what you could be doing in the scene, e.g. woman in the airport departure lounge who keeps asking everyone for their advice because she's never flown before and is scared, *OR* man in the casualty waiting room of the hospital waiting impatiently to see the doctor after hurting his arm somehow.

5. When everyone is in position and ready, the scene-setter-directors shout 'Action' and everyone starts acting in their characters to create a huge class improvisation showing all the things that are going on in different parts of the chosen place or building. You can move from one area to another as you wish – providing it makes sense for your character to do so.

6. After a few minutes the scene-setters-directors shout 'Freeze' and everyone stops acting. They then select one section at a time to show what they've done so far. This will demonstrate how the whole class 'play' is developing from these little scenes.

7. Line up again and ask your teacher to choose a new pair or threesome to be the scene-setter-directors; then try out their ideas for a big class 'scene'.

Headlines

This very easy lesson, which is most suitable for pupils aged 12–16 years, allows pupils to use their imagination to create group improvisations and can be successfully directed by the teacher.

1. Study the newspaper headlines shown overleaf. Try to imagine the stories behind these headlines and make notes showing possible ideas for each one.

2. In groups – choose one of these newspaper headlines and use it as the basis for a fairly lengthy improvisation. You should include more than one scene and give some thought to characterisation as well as 'plot' or storyline. Depending upon your choice of headline, consider carefully the sort of improvisation you want to create. Is it to be a mystery thriller, comedy, serious drama or even a mime?

3. Spend some time practising in your group before possibly showing your work to others in your class.

BANK RAID GOES WRONG

Coins worth 1 Million found in garden

Alien craft sighted on south coast

Millionaire leaves surprise will

THUGS RESPONSIBLE FOR DEATH OF WOMAN — Aged 82

PLANE MISSING — NEAR BERMUDA TRIANGLE!

The Interview

This is a good lesson to use with pupils aged 12–16 years (especially with those approaching leaving age) to introduce 'social drama' and to make them think more carefully about effective characterisation in their plays. Older pupils should be able to work happily on their own but younger pupils may need some help and guidance.

1. *In pairs* – Quickly act out *three* very different interviews. Think about characters; e.g. Teenager with very little to say for him/herself; very confident applicant; someone desperate for *any* job; a friendly interviewer or stern and off-putting interviewer? What type of job is vacant? Is the interview itself an informal or demanding one?

2. *In groups* – Work out at least three different scenes showing what was happening the morning or day before the interview. These scenes should reveal more about the individual characters; their hopes and fears, why they wanted the job, how they knew it was vacant and so on. Think too about reasons for the job being vacant, the interviewer's mood and various causes for this.

3. Now consider carefully the acting you have already done. Have you really built up reality into your characters? Are your scenes really convincing and effective? Is there much walking around or irrelevant dialogue that could be cut out? Alter any parts you feel necessary.

4. Finally – put all your scenes together to create a fairly long and thoughtful play which shows: before the interview; the interview itself and what happens afterwards as well – though not necessarily in that order. You may also decide that showing the *whole* interview scene is not necessary to create the effect you want, in which case showing the waiting room beforehand or just the very end of the interviews might be sufficient.

Don't Just Sit There

Read the first three paragraphs of this valuable lesson to the class, and get their reactions, before starting on item 1. This lesson is probably most suitable for pupils aged 13–16 years, although it can, of course, be used with younger pupils if required, to help them realise the importance of realistic movement in drama work.

One of the most common mistakes pupils make in their drama work is sitting down too long and too automatically! So many potentially interesting improvisations could have been that much better if all the characters didn't spend most of it sitting down! School scenes nearly always end up with pupils sitting talking at desks, yet surely pupils talk while changing for PE, in cookery lessons or while they collect their lunch at the school canteen just as often and these would make for more interesting acting. Family or home scenes are just as bad. It would often appear that mum, dad and children spend every minute *indoors* – sitting at the table or watching TV. In drama sketches important conversations seldom take place on a family outing, with dad under the car or up a ladder or with mum doing anything but the usual ironing, dusting or just sitting down!

Having the main characters in your play sitting down most of the time, whether in the park, at home, in the pub, office, supermarket or school, can be unrealistic and often boring.

Think carefully about the acting you have done in lessons recently – is the above generally true of the drama sketches you have produced?

1. *Get into pairs or small groups* and work out short improvisations involving the following scenes:

a. School scene

b. Home scene

c. A different family scene

d. Scene at work

e. Scene in the supermarket or
    pub

f. Park scene

Try to avoid sitting down. Count the number of times you feel tempted to!

2. *Again in a small group or pairs*

Either: a. Take an idea which you have used in the past and improve it by introducing more action and avoiding too much sitting down.

Or: b. Develop *one* of the scenes given in the first part of the lesson, so that it is both active *and* good.

3. Show any of your improvisations to the rest of the class if you wish but be prepared for them to tell you loudly if they feel you are spending too long sitting down!

Survivor

This is quite a difficult lesson which requires thought and serious acting. It is therefore generally most suitable for older pupils aged 15–16 years but best avoided with any classes that can be 'silly'.

This lesson deals with serious, even tragic drama work so you must concentrate throughout and work very hard to make your acting both convincing and effective.

1. In pairs, act out one of you telephoning the other to give them bad news – gently. What is their reaction?

2. Again in pairs, act out this situation: 'you are both involved in some activity which could be anything from defusing a bomb to watching TV or driving along the motorway. Something happens and one of you is hurt and then dies.' Show the tragic scene and the reaction of the one still alive. Try to keep it as serious as possible, although not necessarily highly emotional.

3. If there is time, remind yourselves of the title 'Survivor' and, in a group, improvise any situation which could be based on this title. It may be in some way connected with the work you have already done or it might be a less depressing interpretation of the word 'Survivor'. You will probably need more than one scene to build up your story and character effectively.

4. Show any of your work if you wish.

Round the Circle

Suitable for all pupils aged 9–14 years, this is an easy lesson to teach.

Both the warm up game and improvisation work afterwards help to promote quick thinking and confidence, as well as being favourites among the pupils.

Warm up game:

1. Ask one pupil to step aside and then divide the rest of the class into pairs. One person from each pair gets a chair and sits in a circle. The partner then stands behind with hands behind his back.

2. Now ask the pupil taken out at the beginning also to get a chair, place it empty in the circle and stand behind it.

3.	The object of the game is for the pupil with the empty chair to 'steal' someone else's partner to sit on his chair. He does this by quickly nodding or winking at someone seated in the circle and thus getting them to run from their chair to his empty one. This leaves the stolen person's original partner with an empty chair and so he, in turn, needs to 'steal' someone else to fill his chair and so on . . .

4.	The seated pupils need to react quickly and move as soon as they are winked at; while the pupil who finds himself with an empty chair in front also needs to act quickly if he is to steal someone else.

5.	Of course, the pupils standing behind the chairs want to prevent their seated partners from being stolen. They must keep their hands behind their backs until they notice their partners being winked at – in which case they prevent them being stolen by swiftly placing their hands on their seated partner's shoulders to stop them getting away. If they succeed, the winker has to try elsewhere – if they fail, they end up with the empty chair!

6.	After a few minutes of playing this game – ask pupils to swop places so that those who have previously been standing now sit on the chairs and vice versa. Remember – one person must start with an empty chair in front.

7.	Play the game for a further few minutes.

Improvisation Work

1.	Ask the pupils who have been standing also to get a chair and join the circle, making sure that they are next to their original partners.

2.	Go round the circle giving each pair a different title, (possible titles are set out below). Tell them they must quickly think up an idea for a very short improvisation based on that title, without leaving their seats or having any chance to practise.

3.	After allowing them only one minute for thought and discussion, ask each pair, in turn, to perform their improvisation/sketch in the middle of the circle. Be warned – they will always think someone else's title is better than theirs and some may be very short and dull indeed, but do not allow anyone to opt out.

4.	Having thus gone right round the circle – remind the class of all the titles that were previously given and tell them they now have the opportunity to pick any one title that they like and think would be good for an interesting improvisation. Again, allow only a minute or two for discussion and working out before going round the circle again seeing their new and improved improvisations.

Possible Titles:

Found	The letter	The exam
Bus stop	Disguise	The joke
The parcel	Spots	Operating theatre
The machine	The problem	Food
Last penny	Accident	Stolen

Five Stages of a Life

This is a lesson which aims to combine drama technique with thoughtful improvisation work. Suitable for ages 12–16.

1. *Concentration/stillness exercise*: Everyone stands in a space, facing a chair which is placed about a foot in front of them. They should stand with legs slightly bent and apart, concentrating on being very still, and gripping the floor as though completely stuck to it. The teacher goes round at random and pushes each pupil from any direction. Only those who remain rock solid are properly concentrating and can therefore sit down. Keep going round until everyone has achieved this. (This is also a very useful exercise for sorting out the silly ones in an unknown class.)

2. *Warm up/preparation*: Again, pupils stand facing their chairs. Tell them to imagine that someone is sitting on the chair in front of them, (think where the head would be). This could be anyone . . . and they are to plead, argue, make fun of or talk to this person. The whole class should start together on the count of three. After about a minute, stop them and ask them to turn their backs on the chair (not too close) and stand perfectly still and solid as before. Once again, go round the room and gently touch the shoulder of a few pupils. When touched, the individual should turn and immediately start talking–rowing with the chair as before. This is obviously more difficult as they are on their own in front of the rest.

3. *Improvisation*: Pupils sit on their chairs while you explain this next part of the lesson and discuss possible ideas or variations. In fairly large groups they stand in a semicircle with their backs to the 'narrator' who tells parts of someone's life story. Five times during the narration members from the semi-circle should turn and act out various important scenes which help develop the character and life of the central person. At the end of each short scene the actors should again turn their backs and the narrator continues. Give plenty of time for these to be worked out and then see one or two.

It All Goes Wrong

Pupils will need little or no help in acting out the simple comedy situations contained in this ever popular lesson for pupils aged 11–16 years.

Work through this sheet, acting out as many of the comedy situations given below as you wish, trying to make each one as funny as possible. If, after doing one or two, you get an idea for a similar comedy sketch of your own, or want to concentrate on one particular idea below, you may, of course, decide to spend more time on that and leave the others. Show any work you wish at the end of the lesson.

1. *In pairs* – one of you is trying to interview a famous sports person or pop star, which is proving very difficult for some reason.

2. *In pairs* – one of you is trying to follow instructions for doing something but having trouble. It might be a television cookery demonstration, a guide to unblocking the drains, a fathers' class for looking after the new baby, a sports lesson or army drill.

3. *In pairs or small groups* – act out a television news broadcast where various things start to go wrong.

4. *In pairs or small groups* – the decorating of a room turns into a mini disaster!

5. *In pairs or small groups* – act out a quick comedy sketch where the spies, burglars or bank robbers just don't seem to be able to get it right.

6. *In pairs or small groups* – an important occasion, e.g. a wedding, seems doomed to failure when it all goes wrong.

Never Say Die

This lesson is suitable for all pupils aged 9–16 years. Although the warm up game may take a few minutes to organise and requires some supervision, it is generally quite straightforward and one which most classes enjoy. The group improvisation work that follows is fairly easy and can produce some quite entertaining sketches.

1. *Warm up:* This drama game – known as 'Wink Murder' or the 'Winking Game' will put you into the right mood for the improvisation work to follow.

Elect a leader:– This may, of course, be the teacher or one of the pupils. Now, all the class stands in a circle except for one person who volunteers to move out of earshot and shut his eyes while the leader chooses one person from the circle to be the 'Murderer'. As everyone in the circle knows who this person is, care must be taken to avoid saying the name or staring too directly at the murderer as this would, of course, then make the guesser's task too easy. The 'guesser' is the person earlier removed from the class who now returns and stands in the middle of the circle.

The 'murderer' tries to 'kill' people in the circle by winking at them in turn, without the guesser noticing. As soon as someone is winked at or 'murdered' in this way, he or she should fall to the ground in truly dramatic fashion. When the 'murderer' has thus 'killed' fifteen people in the circle or the guesser has correctly guessed who the winker is, so the game ends and a new guesser and murderer are chosen.

2.   Go into pairs or groups as you wish and improvise on the idea of someone trying to murder someone else but not succeeding. Each attempt is thwarted in some way, right at the last minute. Depending upon whether you decide to create a horror story, suspense thriller, comedy or serious drama on this theme, the victim may or may not be aware of the attempts being made upon his/her life. Think carefully too about an effective ending. Does the victim get killed or is there a 'twist' in the story? Good timing and careful planning is important throughout.

Take Your Pick

Although this lesson may at first appear complicated, it is, in fact, quite easy to organise and can be used with any pupils aged 9–16 years. You will, ideally, need 3 small containers of some sort (3 chair seats will do if this proves a problem) and quite a bit of rough paper. It saves time if this is already cut into small strips but pupils could do this themselves. Read through the lesson with the class before beginning and then relax as pupils enjoy the challenge to create the most interesting improvisation from their random slips of paper!

1.   Every member of the class needs to have 3 small slips of paper and a pen or pencil. The teacher also needs to provide 3 small containers.

2.   Take the first slip of paper and write a place on it. Try to make it somewhere interesting like 'Halfway up a mountain', or 'In the factory canteen'. Fold the slip so that the writing is hidden and place it in the first container.

3. When everyone has done this, take the second slip and write the name and brief description of a person, e.g. – 'Mark – 17 years old – works at the garage'. Now fold this as before and place in the second container.

4. Again, when everyone has placed their second slips into the container, take the last slip and write down a mood or problem or any extra piece of information, e.g. – 'really fed up' or 'just won the pools' or 'recovering from an operation'. Place these in the last container.

5. Go into groups of 3/4/5. Two people from each group go to the front where the containers are placed and pick out one slip from each container then return to the group. Therefore, each group finally has 2 place slips, 2 character slips and 2 pieces of extra information from which to work.

6. Use all or some of the slips to help you make up an interesting improvisation.

Sculptures (Horror)

Most suitable for pupils aged 10–14 years. You will find that classes love this lesson which helps them appreciate the importance of 'shape' in drama work and further, shows them how atmosphere can be created by using shape, movement and sounds effectively. Some lighting is useful but not essential. Younger groups may need a little help.

1. Get into groups of between 4–8 and then elect a group leader.

2. The leader takes each remaining member of the group in turn and directs them to stand, lie, kneel, stretch or pose in some way; perhaps using a table, blocks, upright or upturned chairs to make their individual positions more dramatic. Slowly the leader builds up an interesting shape or group 'sculpture' from the combined positions of the group members, i.e. one lies back across an upturned chair, another stands leaning menacingly toward him/her while another kneels, terrified, looking upwards with one outstretched arm . . .

3. When the sculpture is complete, the leader then swops places *exactly* with one member of the group thus allowing that member to step back and view the overall shape or sculpture for himself. The leader continues to swop places in this way with all the other members of the group, in turn, so that everyone gets to see the finished sculpture and can suggest any changes needed.

4. Now elect a new leader and start again, building a new and different sculpture using the same method as before and once again, changing places at the end so everyone is able to see and comment upon the completed second sculpture.

5. As a group, decide which sculpture was the best and therefore the one to be used in the next part of the lesson.

6. As you are probably well aware, loudly howling ghosts running around the stage area, witches waving arms about while cackling noisily or Dracula rushing up to his victims shouting 'I'm coming to get you' before sinking his teeth dramatically into their necks, do not really create a true horror scene. It is more likely to make any audience laugh!

   So, get back into positions for whichever of the two sculptures you have chosen and add very *small* movements to it. An occasional turn of the head, just a few fingers moving slowly, a regular tapping of a hand or foot on some surface, an eye winking or both shutting and opening from time to time are all possibilities but there are many more, of course. Be careful not to overdo the movements in your sculpture.

7. Now relax your positions for a minute or two while you decide upon some horror sound effects to go with your sculpture and make it even more sinister. As mentioned before; loud, obvious noises will spoil the effect so think of suitable, soft sounds instead:– e.g. a soft hum, a regular but faint tapping or dripping sound, distant singing of a child's nursery rhyme, an occasional creak or hiss. Remember, you probably won't want everyone making sounds, otherwise it will sound like a discordant orchestra!

8. Get back into your group sculpture using both sounds and movements to create a really eerie scene! Practise once or twice and then tell your teacher when you have finished.

9. When every group is ready, the teacher should ask each group in turn to show their sculpture to the rest. It is a great help if lights can be dimmed at this point to add to the effect.

10. If there is time, work out a horror sketch using some of the ideas given above.

Effects of Mood

This fairly easy lesson develops social awareness through group improvisation work and is suitable for all pupils aged 11 – 16 years. Depending upon the class and situation, sections 2 and 3 may either involve discussion among the pupils in small groups or take the form of class discussion with the teacher.

1. Go into pairs and act out a brief argument: e.g. Why didn't you turn up? You told me lies about –––. Your individual feelings and reasons for the row must be made clear. The argument should also be realistic, with changes in pace, pitch, voice control etc.

2. Sit in a large group and discuss the snowballing effect of someone being in a bad mood, e.g: Mum and daughter have a row at 8.00 a.m. over break-fast –

    > Mum then rows with husband;
    >
    > Daughter is rude to teacher at school;
    >
    > Husband gives secretary sack over silly thing;
    >
    > Teacher argues with another teacher at break;
    >
    > Secretary runs out and gets knocked down by bus;
    >
    > Second teacher hits/picks on pupil who is already upset?
    >
    > etc. etc.

3. Discuss also other ways in which we all influence and affect the lives of others, e.g. drugs, drink, making fun, doing a favour, being forceful, etc.

4. In groups, improvise various scenes to show this snowballing effect and then put them together to form a short play.

5. You may wish to show either your group work or pair work to the others in your class.

Whodunnit?

This is a good light-hearted way of introducing 'role play' and is ideal for allowing the more extrovert members of the class plenty of opportunity to act while the less enthusiastic or shyer pupils can 'sit back' slightly but still be involved. The lesson takes a little time and effort to organise initially but this is worth it as pupils aged 11 – 16 years generally love this lesson and always want to repeat it several times!

1. Divide into groups of preferably four or five. It does not matter if your groups are slightly uneven in number provided each group contains more than three pupils. If possible, you should all have a chair to sit on.

2. One person from each group (the most extrovert?) goes forward and stands in a line at the front. These are to be the 'suspects' in the whodunnit? Those of you who remain in each group should arrange yourselves as a panel with the one empty chair facing you. You are to be the detectives or investigators in the whodunnit?

3. Now you will need to be both patient and quiet while the teacher briefly speaks to the group of suspects somewhere out of earshot, helping them to plan an outline for a whodunnit? The 'suspects' decide who has been killed, how this was done, by whom and why. They then need to take on individual characters, each with a possible motive and opportunity for killing the dead person. Each person quickly works out his/her story ready to give to the panels of detectives, plus any other clues or information they wish to give about other suspects or the dead person. This information may help or mislead the panel, who are trying to solve the murder mystery.

4. They return to the class and tell the rest of you who has been killed and any necessary details like time, place and possibly cause of death, but without giving anything away!

5. Each suspect returns and sits on the chair facing you, the panel. You question this suspect and listen to his/her story, making notes if you wish. The suspect must remember to keep 'in character' throughout.

6. After just a couple of minutes the teacher will call 'change!' Each suspect moves on to be questioned by the next panel or group and, as far as possible, gives much the same story and answers as before.

7. The teacher continues to call 'change!' every few minutes so that the suspects move round to each panel or group in turn being questioned as before.

8. When every panel has had the chance to question all suspects, the suspects return to the front of the class and line up. You will need a few minutes of discussion in your groups so that you can now decide who you think did the deed.

9. Elect a spokesman in each group or panel to announce, in turn, who you think is guilty from the line of suspects and how you have reached this decision. You may wish the suspect in each case to step forward.

10. Finally, the *real* murderer steps forward and reveals him or herself to the class. There may, of course, have been more than one person involved. How many of you got it right?

11. Start a new whodunnit? with a new set of suspects if there is time.

John

A very easy lesson for any teacher to take, this work is most suitable for pupils aged 14–16 years who are required to use their skill, insight and imagination to create a series of group improvisations based on a central character. Pupils who wish to alter the passage slightly or want to concentrate on just one section rather than acting out the whole speech should be allowed to do so.

1. Read the following passage. John casually describes himself and his situation after leaving school six months ago. His account has deliberately been left vague and incomplete so that you can form your own impression of his character and what he is doing now.

   'Hi – my name's John. I left school six months ago and look at me now! School, that's a laugh! They say school is the best years of your life – well all I remember about school was ....

   Mum thought I should be an accountant or dentist or something. You know what Mums are like. Full of little dreams for their precious children. Accountant? Me?! That just shows how little she really knows me. My dad? Now there's a different story again – I mean, that time I ....

   Thinking about school again, though, you know I haven't really kept in touch with anyone from there. We all went our different ways – thank goodness! There were some really funny characters in my year – take Sarah Smith and Tom Hedges for instance. I can just see them now ....

   I still see Dave, though. Only last week he phoned and ....

   Anyway, here I am. John, you've come a long way in six months, I must say. Still, can't spend all day talking to you. (*Turns away*).

   Well, Joe. What do you think ....,'

2. You will have noticed that some sentences end with a dotted line. Remembering that there is more than one way of interpreting John's character and situation, start to think of interesting scenes which could be

shown where the dotted lines appear. The main character could just as easily be a girl, of course.

3. In groups, act out John's whole speech, replacing the dotted lines with interesting and convincing scenes which help build up a clear picture of John and other characters. Decide where he is when making this speech.

4. Practise this a few times and then perhaps show the rest of the class what you have done.

Court Case

Classes usually work well in this lesson which combines the use of slightly different drama techniques with characterisation to create interesting and thoughtful group improvisations. Most suitable for pupils aged 13–16 years, therefore you may wish to omit some sections if younger pupils find it difficult to finish in the time available; and it is probably wise to read the lesson through with the class to make sure they really understand it before going off into their groups.

This improvisation work helps you to develop characters properly as well as using 'flashbacks' to create an interesting court scene.

1. Get into a group of 4, 5 or 6. Think about a courtroom scene and what sort of characters might be present.

    1a. *The teacher here explains the nature of the various people in a Crown Court – Judge, Clerk of Court, Accused, Counsel (both sides), Jury – and their functions.*

2. Decide which people of the group are going to be which characters and give each one a definite personality and background. For example: the judge may have his mind on a money problem or a coming holiday. He might be getting a bit tired of sitting in court day after day and need a rest. Perhaps he really wanted to be a vet when he was younger but something went wrong . . .

3. Get a chair each and sit in a line. One by one turn towards an imaginary audience and start talking to them about yourself, your life and why you are sitting outside the courtroom. Remember to keep in character while doing this. The others in the line must remain perfectly frozen until it is their turn to speak.

4. Now, act out any courtroom scene you wish, dealing with any kind of court case, e.g. a stolen car. Think carefully about the characters as well as creating an interesting storyline. This may be serious or comedy work depending upon the talents of your group.

5. Now act out the same court scene as before but this time use the idea of actors freezing while one character tells 'his story' to the audience, just as you practised at the beginning of the lesson. Obviously this need not be done sitting in a straight line this time, but the same insight into the characters' backgrounds, feelings and personalities should be shown. You will probably find that not all characters will need to do this – depending upon their part in the play.

6. Try using 'flashbacks' as well to help build up a fuller picture of what has happened in the lives of certain characters and how the court case was caused. It can sometimes prove more interesting for an audience to be shown the most important or even the last scene of a play first, while being told the full story, bit by bit, in a series of flashbacks – rather than watching one scene after another, set in the proper order, very gradually building up the play.

7. Working out your final play will take some thought and time but when you feel you have finished you may wish to show this to the rest of the class. If you have done it properly it should prove to be an interesting and worthwhile performance whether in the form of comedy or serious acting.

Expression

Pupils usually enjoy this fast-moving and fun lesson which helps them appreciate the importance of expression and tone of voice in drama work and is most suitable for pupils aged 14–16 years.

The following drama improvisation work is meant to help you realise how even very simple phrases and sentences can be said in a variety of ways, each one giving it a slightly different meaning. This, in turn, will help you when you read from written plays or perform future improvisation.

1. In pairs – use the phrase 'I've got it' in five different, extremely short scenes. The phrase should be said in a different way – suggesting a different meaning each time.

2. Now do the same thing again with each of the following phrases:

    a. I don't know.

    b. Oh dear.

    c. It's a shame.

    d. Excuse me.

3. Keeping in your pair – work out a short improvisation which uses either 'Oh Henry' or one of the above phrases again, in as many different ways as you can manage. Remember, it will take you a few minutes to think of just one scene which will include all these interpretations, and still make some sense!

4. Now think of any phrase, word or sentence you wish and work out an ordinary drama sketch of any kind using only that phrase as speech throughout. Your phrase could, for example, be 'eggs and bacon' and you might decide to act a hospital scene saying only eggs and bacon all the way through, but showing what you really mean by the tone of your voice and the expression that you give it. If you are stuck for ideas you could perhaps use a sketch you have already worked out in a previous drama lesson as the basis for this.

5. If there is time, experiment with the idea of expression of voice a bit further or, if you wish, show any of your perhaps amusing scenes to the rest of the class.

Lesson Completion Chart

LESSON	CLASS	DATE

LESSON	CLASS	DATE

LESSON	CLASS	DATE

LESSON	CLASS	DATE